Grey Area Currency

Rebirth of Pearl Security

Anthony V. Jones Sr.

Grey Area Currency

Rebirth of Pearl Security

Blanco Court Publishing

Corpus Christi, Texas

Grey Area Currency

Copyright@ 2020 Anthony V. Jones Sr.

ISBN: 978-0-578-73026-4

I dedicate this book to my wife, Linda L. Saenz

Jones. Without you my life would not be well lived and

my heart full. You have pushed and prodded me to

get me to this first book.

Thank you and love you forever!

Introduction

Needless to say as the team is pinned down by the suppressing fire of the Orethian gangsters there is a fleeting thought of surrender. However, being taken, tortured then killed only three weeks into a 24 month contract is actually a waste of good flesh. Being killed and not getting paid at the 12 month mark is absolutely stupid!

The smell of Orethians in the air even through the filtered masks, leaves the team gasping. Orethians bodies produce an overwhelming putrid smell when they sweat. It is a combination of sulphur, vomit and rot.

A look at the surroundings the team is pinned down in what is left of the gambling hall in the basement of Saractac Towers in Oleo Springs Township in Greygo City. Placing all caution to the wind the team attacked to save two of their allies. The firefight and its ongoing barrages has at least 20

Zinghavis dead intermingled with the roasted carcasses of 15 Orethian hit squad members.

Pinned down and still heavy on ammo the team waits on orders from their leader Ronald Cashmere, who is pinned down as the Zinghavi assailants continue to fire their older but powerful weapons at his position. His combat suit is covered in remnants of two hit squad members who he is using as cover behind the Orethian version of a blackjack table. On his signal she hand gestures the return assault play from the vast playbook of Pearl Security. All communications are jammed due to the floating masses of metal chips suspended in a magnetic halo grenade fields.

Flanking right and left respectively, Carla "Flips" Jefferson and Shawn King scuttle around bodies and overturned tables to provide the pincers in the trident formation. Backing them from a higher vantage point behind them, Rodrigo "Rod" Matta is setting up grenade launcher with phosphorous loads to melt and blind to push the hit

squad into the vice. Ronald's hand counts down to one...

Part 1

Chapter 1

A Right Tussle

The winger sets hard against the right side of the pitch and waits for the striker to slice into the box. Score being nil this is the part of the match where every gambler in London has his note gripped tightly, because they could be rich or poor on this cross. Winger hits the cross and it curves towards the net and the striker has the right angle. A horn blows and he looks up. He raises the bar at the parking booth and turns his attention back to the screen.

"Offside! Are you bloody serious?" Ronald groans as the 200 pound gambling note burns a hole in his breast pocket.

Ronald "Cash" Cashmere Jr. is the last remaining vestige of the Pearl Security Consultants. The company was started by his great grandfather after World War 2 as water front security for importers and exporters. He grew it to a substantial business and expanded into personal security then armored cars. This was a grand accomplishment for an immigrant from West Africa. Following that trajectory the business was supposed to maintain the family for generations, until it fell into the spastic hands of his two sons, Ronald Cashmere and Donald Cashmere his twin brother. The luck of the two combined was worse than zero! Ill-fated marriages coupled with illicit vices corrupted the family enterprise as one client after another bailed to another company who didn't ask for advances or turned their eyes to the subversive bootlegger. Between the two only one sired a son, Ronald "Cash" Cashmere III and left him with one contract, a parking garage in the East End.

As the match continues, Cash is fixated as the to and fro of the match further intensifies the possibility of getting a win today. Sporadic traffic gives him lulls in the access to the

garage where he sees and feels the burning of the note turn

to ice as the Devils score. The luck of the Cashmere name

does not disappoint as he loses again. As the street lamps

flicker to life and he waits for his son, Ronald the IV to show

up for the evening shift. He contemplates any idea to get his

son and himself out of the drafty box earning just enough to

pay the taxes on the family home in Shore Ditch.

Young Ronald shows up and is the spitting image of

his Pop. Tall, lean and muscular with sprinkles of white in his

beard and hair. The older Cashmere had lost his hair early

and keeps his melon clean shaven with more invasive white in

his beard.

"Evening, Pop." He says as he drops his lunch sack and

thermos on the small desk under the booth window. His

hands are a combination of scars and calluses from his day

job of laying bricks for the construction companies of the new revitalized area of the city. He is all in with his Pop and pitches in every quid to help.

"Evening. Been pretty slow today. The Whites let us down again."

"I saw. Maybe next time." As he puts his hand on his Pop's shoulder as the elder continued to be seated. The strain of not winning and being limited to this six by six box has worn him down over the years.

"Okay. See you in the morning..." Cash says as his voice trails off. The sound of sirens and gunfire captures their attention as both their heads whip around to the North. Through the roundabout comes three motorcycles with two riders apiece. The rear riders were firing machine guns at pursuing police. As the firefight heads their way the duo leave the booth and seek cover in the garage. The lead cycle heads in the direction of the garage and blows in through the exit side followed by the other two. The police cars stop and

7

block the entry and exit. All three cycles head up the circular

drive upwards at a great rate of speed. There is a crash and

an explosion as two bodies roll back in flames followed by a

separate explosion that cracks the lower driveway.

Cash curses and Ronald groans as they both see their

source of income being decimated before their awestruck

eyes. Both of them shake their heads from the shock and

look at each other with grim determination. They give each

other a nod and pull their own weapons, twin 40 caliber

pistols. The father and son grew up and were raised in Shore

Ditch after all. Both slither towards the stairwell not wanting

to be shot by the police after all. Once getting into the

stairwell they bound up each floor and checking the levels

through a cracked door with no success, until deck 5.

Ronald spies the four remaining hoods checking car

doors for an escape. They split up into two man teams and

go in opposite directions. Each pair carries a black duffel and two grenades.

"They got grenades, Pop. That is what blew up ground deck."

"So what are they doing now?" As Cash dabs the sweat from his brow. There is a twinkle in his eye as his adrenaline pumps through his now reawakened heart. Exhaustion is replaced with it and he is ready.

"Split up to the east and west. You go east and I take west?" Ronald says with a grin and heads to the left without waiting for a response. He takes cover behind a BMW and glides effortlessly between the bumpers and outside wall. The walls being concrete obstructs views from the street.

Cash heads right and is not as stealthy. He strides slightly bent at the waist heading at an angle cutting across the wide open spaces, gun at the ready. Sneaking around on his own property will not happen. The first shot shatters a windshield to his right and he tucks and rolls to his left. He does not return fire. Why waste a shot if he can't see them. Wait till they come to check and gloat then give them a gift.

Ronald freezes as he hears the three shots, but no return fire. His blood runs cold as the possibility of Pop being killed. The anger fills his mind and eyes with a rage that will wink out the souls of these four men today! Ronald continues to move and gradually using car windows to locate the first two hoods before they escape. As he gets to the end of the row he sees them placing the bags into the back of a black Rover. They have not caught sight of him yet and he contemplates who to get first. Chance upon chance the taller of the two gets in the Rover under the dashboard to try to get the truck started. That leaves the smaller one to head in his direction to apparently check for the police. Ronald seizes the opportunity and slides back to the far side of the car he is already using for cover.

"I can't believe this easy job turned out like this. Eddie and Yez are dead..." the hood says as he peeks over the wall. The street below is crawling with cops. Then all of a sudden the cops are getting closer and he can't scream as the ground comes up to meet him. Ronald slides to the rear of the car thief as his partner becomes a hood ornament.

Chapter 2

Statement

The click of the hammer freezes the hood and Ronald waits. He can see each of his hands and there is no gun visible.

"Get up. Nice and slow." Ronald tells him and moves to his right to avoid getting hit with the truck door. The guy is pretty tall when he stands up and is full head taller than Ronald at 6'2". How in the world was this bloke on a motorcycle? He is standing there with motorcycle mask covering the bottom of his face. His eyes are searching for his partner and Ronald sees the smug smile crinkle his green eyes.

Ronald smiles and pretends to look over his shoulder then smiles.

"Oh, you looking for your short partner?" He says while he moves his right hand approximately parallel to his gun hand.

The big man's eyes flash with fear and his hands tremble. He takes a step forward. Ronald fires two shots into his chest and the shots blow him back into the open truck door. However, the big man uses the door as a catapult and launches himself at Ronald. A bulletproof vest...

After the shock of the attack wears off. Ronald realizes not only is he is tall, but is very strong. The gun flies out of his hand and not even in play. He feels the three right hands in succession catch him under his arms into his ribs. This is followed by a left uppercut aimed at his face. Ronald leans into the man's body and the blow contacts his upper chest. Body shots robbing him of his wind, Ronald drives a knee to his body aiming for the bullets entry and is rewarded by the whoosh of air as the man crumples. This has helped

13

him to get the upper hand in the brawl as it continues with

massive punches and legs making contact. In reality a real

street fight last a few minutes not all day like in the movies.

After a hard elbow to the back of the hood's neck, he goes

limp. Ronald staggers around looking for the gun and finds it.

His eye is swollen shut and his nose is bleeding, but

other than that it is just bruises. He is out cold, but he has no

cuffs or anything to tie him up. He could shoot him? There is

a better idea. He finishes starting the Rover and backs the

truck over his arm.

"Can't leave without the arm." Ronald mumbles to

himself as he looks at his brown skin and the swelling. He

makes his way to the trunk and is curious what is in the bags.

As he opens the trunk he knows he has to hurry. Opening the

first bag he sees the stacks of pounds and the same in the

second bag.

Meanwhile, on the opposite side of the garage Cash is crawling between the cars trying to prepare himself for the hoods. While he is crawling he sees the booted feet of two people, two cars over. He hears them talking, but can't hear what they are saying. Since he is down here, he might as well. Cash takes two quick shots and makes one count. One of the hoods drops and curses as his shin is broken. The bag he is carrying is blocking his upper body, so Cash gets up and shuffles away as the other hood pulls his partner to cover.

Cash meets them and has them dead to rights. The injured hood is covered with the heavy duffel and the one standing has his hands stuck under his armpits.

"Okay what do you want old man?" The shot one moans as his leg continues spurting through the split above his ankle.

"Really? You are in my garage, bleeding all over my lot. Then you insult me?"

15

Cash's bald head is gleaming from the sweat and adrenaline starting to wear off. His baby blue work shirt is drenched and the drama is over.

"You two keep your hands up and out where I can see him."

Cash begins to back away and checking behind him as he leaves. Retreating in this fashion he waits for Ronald to show up. He heard the two shots and knows his son came out on top. Nothing imitates the sound of a 40 caliber striking home. The two hoods continue to stand with their hands out. The motorcycle masks hide everything but their eyes. Both of them are Caucasian as their red and blonde hair respectively falls below their helmets. Cash keeps his retreat until he finds partial cover behind the Peugeot to his right. There he settles in and waits for Ronald to show up. As he looks back at his agitators, he looks past them over the side of the garage and sees all the pulsating lights. He hears the squawk and static of the radios. Cash knows that the coppers will be moving in soon and he and Ronald need to get out of the way.

"Hey! You with the hole in his leg. What's in the bag?" Cash asks. The injured man glowers at him as the sweat and tears cover his masked face. His partner has laid him down and is calculating a way to get out.

"What's it to you!" The injured man grunts out as he collapses from the loss of blood.

"Look here. Its money and a lot of it. You let us go or better yet hide us, a bag is yours." The standing one blurts out as the sound of boots are reverberating from the stairway.

"We could take the bag and leave you for the coppers anyway!" Ronald says as he jogs up. The relief is apparent on both father and son.

"Pop. Those bags have a lot of money, but you know these "geniuses" did not come up with this plan on their own. So whoever paid them for this job will be looking for this money. It's tempting, but not worth the risk." Ronald says as he looks around nervously as the boots get closer.

While both men are contemplating what to do next. The standing criminal makes a decision for all of them. He pulls a grenade and holds the pin between his teeth. As the release clangs to the ground, all eyes focus on it. The tall man smiles and closes his eyes. Ronald grabs Cash and they run to their right to put cars between them and the explosion. The concussive force catches and propels them forward at the same time as the coppers clear the stairway. As the debris and cars continue to explode, father and son tuck and roll behind a half wall. Within the debris pounds are fluttering among the flames and smoke. After the last explosion there is a crack and a shudder as fifth deck tilts towards the street as the pillars give way on the street side. The groaning and cracking continue as debris starts to land on the police barricade. Cops scramble and the chaos continues as the dust plume rises above the structure.

Cash and Ronald remained huddled together as they slide with the tilting garage waiting for the explosion aftermath to finally stop. As they are rolling the roll over the fissure that has transected the fifth deck. They both land in a heap on the street side off the garage amid the alarms of cars as they too crash and grind into each other as well. Cops bound onto the garage deck not only to make an arrest it is to avoid the rocking stairway. As they spread out they find Cash and Ronald staggering towards them.

"Halt!" Three cops in tactical gear point their weapons at the father and son. In unison they both raise their hands, place them behind their heads and kneel with a sigh. Cuffs are locked and they are separated and escorted from the garage. They are taken downstairs and placed in separate cars and taken in to the police station. Cash peers over his shoulder and looks at his only business in smoking ruins.

"Hey, which station are you taking me too?" Cash asks as he tries to get comfortable with the grit and dust causing his neck and shoulders itch.

"The Bow!" The cop growls in frustration. He continues to drive as down Grove Road.

As the lights and noise recede as they leave, a figure watches from an upper window of the flat across the street. They are obscured by the drapes, but a feathered hand rests on the sill and they emit a purring sound of satisfaction.

Chapter 3

In a Crack

Five years earlier the visitor came from somewhere and that somewhere was the planet of Orenthia located in the Andromeda Galaxy on the cusp of its outer edge nearest to the Milky Way's edge. It is in rotation around a dwarf star named Miriam and orbits it on a 10 month orbit. Oddly it has an anomaly not present in the solar system of Earth, it is tethered to another planet by gravitational pull, Zinghavi. The tether and the planet have been this way for tens of millions of years. The "umbilical" between the planets have trapped space transients into this field and has formed a hardened passage between the worlds called the "Transient". The Transient has no atmosphere and neither planet is able to close off access to the other with barriers, however each has monitors to see who comes and goes.

As two planets go there are vast differences and only one similarity they have learned to communicate. This communication in the view of the Zinghavians is that of a prisoner in a palace. There are no limits to comfort, but they are still a prisoners. Once each race had their diverse ways of living. The Zinghavians are technologically one of the most advanced in the galaxy, but that intellect does nothing when it comes to physical combat or all-out war. In an effort to prevent a loss of their planet and all of their riches. They formed a beneficial alliance in a sense with the Orethians. The Orethians are a battle hardened species living in harsh conditions on their own home world. Their tenacity in battle and pure savagery has kept many other races away from their world. This helped in two major attempts and they were pushed back. The Orethians were provided weapons and short transports to fulfill the protection obligation and the Zinghavians were always ready to provide. However, the Orethians discovered not only they were stronger than their benefactors, they also realized the toil of their current lives on their own planet would be much easier if they dominated their weaker partner in the alliance.

Zinghavi is a planet that is rich in mineral deposits and covered in a majority of water as Earth. However the land masses are mountainous that over the centuries the cities were developed as floating platforms that tethered to the mountainous ranges. The industries for mineral mining and power sourcing happen under water away from the cities. So there is separation in the capacity the cities thrive as entertainment, family living and recreation. The cities themselves are high rise buildings made of phez. Phez is a mineral deposit found in the ocean at the southern hemisphere. As a metal it is ultra-lightweight, however it has the tensile strength of titanium. This allows the platforms to maintain balance above the ocean's surface.

Zinghavians over the centuries evolved from previous stature in terms of bodies. Early Zinghavians were short and hands and feet webbed, however after so many centuries

living on the platforms the webbing had dissolved and their

frame has become more bulbous. Their skin more correctly

described as fine feathers remain, such as those of penguins.

Bone density is higher due to the movement of living on a

floating surface for centuries.

Chapter 4

It Pays to Be Smart

As Ool lays in his sleep chamber and stares at the peak of his greater toe of his webbed foot over his pronounced belly, he has an idea. The tumbling and bumbling from his sleep chamber as it rotates in his bedroom on its gimbals and maintain stability. Ool as the President's advisor never slept, but spent his nights and mornings trying to fix his planet's problems. The problems are many and some much sharper and deadlier than most. Majority of the issues all point down the waste tube of the tether to Orenthia.

Finally, getting to his feet after getting the chamber to settle into wake mode. Wake mode always seem too bright for his pre-naturally hooded eyes that never fully evolved to full light. The face fully resembles that of Alithian lizard, the horned nose and red eyes with conical protruding eyes. As he waddles to the bathing chamber the floor lights up as he takes his steps. Lights are lower to de-sensitize lighting to a

Zinghavians senses. Upon reaching the bathing chamber, he

removes his night shirt and steps in the bathing tube. Once

the door seals, he is plunged to the ocean where his body

absorbs the minerals and each breath his reservoir fills to

carry him through the day.

After the return to his pod, he has to primp and preen

his feathers and layer on the moisturizing salve to protect his

skin. Tunic and kilt straightened, he heads to the kitchen for

breakfast of Malok berries and shiners (small moss fish). Now

to his idea, he makes the call to Tul. Tul is not only his best

friend, but the purveyor of everything black market and

illegal. As the call bingles and bongles he continues to

wonder if he is mad. Finally, the hologram screen fills with

Tul with a splash of glitter and a receding webbed hand and

shells on their nails.

"What do you want Ool!" Tul says as he swipes lip

paint from his mouth.

"Well, well, my friend…Did not know you were so busy?" Ool says with a laugh.

"Okay, what is it?"

"I need a favor. Is it possible for you to get me into the Communications History Wing in Boola province?"

"What for?"

"I have an idea to get us some help against Orethian infection. We need some help and we have to get it from somewhere else."

This idea of help gets Tul up and he fumbles around and falls out of view. There is crashing and a scream. Followed by papers flying past the camera.

"Okay, you have my full attention. I have a couple of Orethian outlaws that hate Desert King. It will cost a lot, but they are worth it."

"No. They will only bleed us for the money and then join them for our punishment for fighting back. I am talking off world, off world. Remember when we were kids and we

27

went on that field trip to the History Wing. We saw the Earth satellite thing with those moving pictures. They were great warriors!"

"Are you dried out? That was over 30 cycles ago. It was a movie called Magnificent something?"

Tul strokes his chest feathers as he rocks in his chair. Quietly and rhythmically he starts to bob his head with an idea, but suddenly stops.

"Wait what is the whole idea before I decide to help you and that's it."

Ool has not verbalized the whole idea except to his toes and the recharge in the shower. How can he explain this to Tul and not get undercut by Tul's greed.

"Well I'm waiting..." Ool says as he disappears off camera again and he hears the cooing of the unseen lady. As Ool is about to attempt to disconnect.

"Don't you dare? Spill it!"

"First, get me in and I will know if the plan will even work." Ool hoped this bluff will give him enough time to make sure it is possible. The funding and contacts will have to be built plus who can he trust for the long term.

There is a long moment of hesitation and Tul shrugs his shoulders.

"Fine I will get you in, but once you get what you want. I get first access. Deal?"

"Deal." As Ool smiles inwardly.

"Meet me out front in one sharkoo (hour). I will be there."

After the holo call disconnected. Ool holo calls the Quorum of Legacy and tells them that he won't be in today. He thinks about everything he needs and prepares himself for the salvation of his planet.

Tul slipping Ool in was a simple payoff to the security to let them in while he ate a bowl of leecher worms. The problem was shaking Tul and his bodyguards so Ool can find what he is looking for. The Earth files from the satellite are in a language that is easy enough, but reading the language is another issue. In a work around he downloaded a screener program that can decipher the written form of the language. The only problem is that what he needs is at the end. Tul will not be patient enough to watch the whole thing without pestering him.

He only needs one thing and it will make their life so much easier. They make their way to the lift and make it to the visual vault. Going through the vault he finds the silver disc. Going to the player he is followed by Tul.

"Ool, what is really going on?"

"What are you talking about? Just researching some information and trying to get our planet free."

"So how are you going to do that? Plus, how much currency will you ask the President for?"

"Tul, why? You cannot beat the Orethians. No one on this planet can defeat them. So no matter what we are in the same boat. The deal that our forefathers made put us here.

Anyone else is going to present us with the same danger. So

what is your better idea?"

Tul looks intently at Ool and his crown feathers begin

to tinge pink in the escalation of anger. Absently he pulls a

shresh blade from his pocket and flicks it back and forth. Ool

sees the anger building, but he cannot back down now.

"Okay. I need a name so I can make a contact on

Earth. It is exactly half an evolution (six months) from here.

They are not from our galaxy and their intrusion will not

cause punishment to us."

"Sounds bizarre, but how much money are you

offering? Tul says as his bodyguards close the doors.

"Don't know. However, there are more pressing

issues and you with your muscle pressing me will get us

nowhere."

Tul mulls this over and puts his blade away. Flicking

his cuffed and jeweled hand to the door and then all three

leave. There is no response or retort leaves Ool a little cold.

He has to work fast, because something is wrong, very wrong.

Tul is connected and has some nefarious connections with

our Orethian partners. As in any society the lure of women,

drugs and money are universal. He inserts the disc into the

player and the movie begins. As the movie rages on the

humans and strange beasts battle the other faction of beasts.

The one in black directs and guides the others into the battle.

Strange how humans differ, one is dark, one has different

eyes and one is huge. Differences such as these are not

normal in the Zinghavi race. As the battle reaches its climax

and there are explosions everywhere there is small rumble

that vibrates through Ool's seat.

The script has finally started scrolling on the screen.

Rumbles are still coming in an intermittent lapses. This

cannot be good. Ool hooks up his data retrieval device to pull

the needed data. The download is registering and the

deciphering program continues pulling the data and he reads

to see if he finds the key word. It starts with the "letter" that

has opposing humps in the line. His eyes focus for that

symbol and then the rumble turns to a groan as the whole

the History Wing jolts from the shock. Ool runs to the

window and wants to see the cause of the disruption. There

on the steps of the Museum there is a squad of Orethians

firing explosive projectiles against the shuttered doors.

"Frazz! This is not a coincidence. Tul sold me out!"

Running and looking through the door to the chamber

there is not anyone around. All the glow rods are turned off

and the blackness has a feel of tragedy forthcoming. The

booming reverberates throughout the halls and rattles to his

pin feathers. Ool heads back and checks the screen for the

opposing line symbols. It is there and his device pulls the

data that he needs, although he cannot pronounce it. The

symbols are; Pearl Security Agency. He unplugs the device

and places it in his tunic inner pouch and ejects the disc.

Upon leaving the room he hides the disc in chloraball

chamber game. It is rounds stones with different sizes that have to be pushed in a hole on opposite ends.

Escape was already planned in preparation of this potential and active double cross. The hoots and howls of the Orethian gang echoes up to the wing he is currently in. Leaving the chamber he makes the right turn and runs for the side exit behind the recharging chambers. What a lot of Zinghavi citizens know is that the recharging tubes do not open into the oceans, but are pressurized with the water. However, if the tube is pressurized with the floor closed the pressurization pushes a citizen up. Ool reverses the system and is ejected to the maintenance tube on the roof. Once on the roof he heads to the opposite side of the roof away from the front of the museum that angles toward the cushion car dealership. The rumbling underfoot spurs him to the edge where Ool vaults over the side of the building and bloats his chest for the impact.

Chapter 5

Duck and Run

Ool hits the roof and bounces then rolls and expels the air from his chest chamber and lays there. Allowing the dizziness to pass he lies between two cushion cars. He is jarred from his shock with howls and hoots from the window level with his landing spot at the parking pad. Projectiles start pinging off of the surrounding vehicles so he gets up and starts to run. The gang has to come down then up since their large frames cannot fit through Orenthia windows. This does not deter the shots from coming and spurring his escape.

Hitting the ramp Ool runs using the downward momentum to get more speed. Hopefully, his planning has afforded him the time to get to the cushion cycle hidden on the back of the building. He bumps and crashes along the hallway trying to find a way down to the street before the gang catches him and Tul gets this information to exploit. As he careens around a corner he sees a ramp heading down. The data on his device is motivation and he churns his legs and hits the door with urgency. As he hits the street the first phase of his escape is there. It is a benefit being a Zinghavians and that is they are an identical species. What sets them apart is their dress. Fifteen Zinghavians are standing in a group outside the door with the same color tunic on. Once he merges into the group the split up into four different directions.

There are choruses of shouts and growls as the Orethians see their quarry multiply and disperse. Not knowing what to do they split up as well to follow each group? Once the group turns the corner, two of the imposters hop on cushion cycles and leave. They two go in two separate directions at a high rate of speed leaving their pursuers dumbfounded and left behind. Ool witnesses this as he sits next to his boss, Lintoo, Quorum Chief.

"Were you successful?" Lintoo asks.

"Yes. Success but not without the pain." Ool says as he sees all the missing feathers along his arm and torn tunic. He pulls the device from his pocket and it is fully intact. All this trouble means he cannot return home since he know they will be waiting.

"Lintoo...I can't stay here." He says as the cushion car continues making random turns throughout the city. Thinking about it the best place is on a ship to where the help will be. This is the time to get the plan together.

"Lintoo, the plan is this. I want to contact an Earth security force and use them as a surgical strike force. They will not patrol the streets as enforcers, but they can hit the Orethians at their strongholds and free our planet."

"What about Ash?"

"Ash?"

Both sit in silence as they both ponder the leader of the Orethians. Ash is somewhat a myth or nightmare. It leads the Orethians as over encompassing wave that devours everything in its wake. But, more recently Ash has them

infecting the planet as well placed infections that have not

taken over. In reality they have formed disruption that keeps

citizens afraid and them living luxuriously in their midst.

"Lintoo that is a large order, but it will be the ultimate

goal."

"How much currency will you need?"

"Lintoo, I fully don't understand their currency, but at

least let me get to their universe and tap their feeds. I will

have a better idea then. As for now could you get me to the

space port in Ragul? I have a ship there and bags just in case

this happened with a team to assist me."

"Not a problem, but you have to let me know quickly.

You will be listed as missing to keep them off balance."

"Thank you."

The rest of the trip is made in silence. Broadcasts are

airing over the car's system speaking of the chaos in the

Boola province. Many Orethians are afraid and damage to

the Wing is extensive. At the end of the broadcast there is an announcement of a missing Zinghavian called Ool. They both smile to themselves and ride to the port.

Upon reaching the ship the pull under the shadow of the ship before he leaves the car. Before leaving the frequencies and times of communication are established. Lintoo hands Ool thirty pound bag of jewels. Ool opens the bag that is teeming with clear crystals, red and green gems are mixed in with them as well.

"This should at least shorten the time to get an agreement. The cost of our freedom is worth way more than this."

"I will be successful." Ool says as he exits the vehicle and enters the ship. The doors close and the ship powers into the upper atmosphere on its mission. As the burst through the upper atmosphere they turn to wormhole AB3. Ool sees the Umbilical and their Sun through the window portal. His home he is leaving to an unknown on his own gamble. The sadness threatens to consume him, but the freshness of the

scars of his escape remind him of why. He slowly fingers the

raw wounds of abrasions of his escape. The true hurt is not

of the wounds, but the betrayal of Tul that truly hurts.

Knowing that his "friend" is in bed with the Orethians

cements his thoughts to this mission.

He goes to the desk and turns on the computing

device that he packed in his own belongings. This system will

be isolated so no one can see his work. Plugging in his device

the program starts to interface with the vocalization and the

system helps him understand what he is seeing.

As the system vocalizes he understands that the word

is Security and the name underneath is Pearl Security

Consultants. This gives him the direction who to look for.

Now he waits as the rest of the program breaks down the rest

of the data. Earth operates in paper currency and a

substance called gold. The language was not that

complicated to vocalize their language with his own chords.

The hours and months he mastered the language and a loose

plan of how to approach the Pearl Security Consultants. The

destination being a place called London.

Chapter 6

Pinkie

Dolores Savage sits at her desk in her sitting room in her regally appointed home in Camden, Northwest side of London. As she tends to her morning tea, she watches the mayhem that happened at a parking garage in the East End. The anchor drones on about explosions and ties it into the robbery of Reserve Bank of Australia near Lothbury. The spoon continues to make its circular route without any break. Her face in its reddish hue shows no inflection or emotion, which unnerves her guest.

Gus sits there waiting for his punishment for the botched robbery. A simple smash and grab leaves five of his crew dead and one in with the butcher getting his broken elbow and arm set. Thirty million pounds reduced down to five million pounds, which means twenty-five million pounds of punishment awaits him. As he does the arithmetic in his head the spoon has stopped stirring and those cold eyes finally focus on him.

"Now Gus. Please, explain to me how you lost 25 million pounds?" Dolores asks in her even tone with the inflections of her Indian descent. Dolores is the youngest daughter of Ricard Savage the Opium King of New Delhi. All of his children were dispersed all over the world and Dolores got the United Kingdom. She is a solid woman that is hidden underneath her tailored suits and flowing raven hair with light streaks of gray. If she was not the Princess of the underworld, she would be the CEO of any company.

"Ma'am...The plan was executed as planned, but the coppers showed sooner than planned. The blokes pressed us off the exit route and the alternate was jammed as well. So they improvised..." Gus stutters and mumbles.

"Improvisation is for performers, actors and children. Are you my child?" Dolores asks still even toned and takes a sip of her tea while never breaking her gaze from him. Gus is

43

ten years older than Dolores and the road this conversation is taking is tightening his gut.

"No I am not. Then again all I can get out of Sven is about the garage attendant. Says he shot him and got the upper hand. He underestimated them and so did the others."

"Well...Improvisation leads to assumptions and assumption leads to me missing 25 million pounds!" She screams and continues to sip her tea.

Her scream brings in her personal guards. They both are over six feet and built like refrigerators. Their eyes have no emotion, but they both await orders to either attack or kill. This is a thin line that Gus isn't sure what would be better.

"The Cashmeres are not docile or timid. I looked into them. They only own that garage, because of mismanagement of the deceased brother. Who would not be perturbed if the only income is being blown up and shot up by a crew that lost 25 million pounds?" She says as she makes eye contact with the first bodyguard, Randall. He grabs a tea cup and a cigar cutter.

"So they are the Cashmeres?" He asks just to buy himself more time as he stares at the cigar cutter.

"Oh yes. They are a tough lot. The one that ventilated and broke up Sven is Ronald Cashmere III. Royal Marine veteran and the son of Ronald "Cash" Cashmere Jr who in turn was tough bloke in his youth as well. A father and son devoured up and spit out your crew that lost my 25 million pounds." She says and stands up to smooth her suit jacket and place her tresses in a ponytail. As she makes her way around the table to Gus the second bodyguard clamps Gus around his left arm and straddles that arm and head. As Gus struggles the behemoth squeezes.

"Sit still now Gus." Dolores purrs as she puts on her apron. The first bodyguard places the teacup in his palm and positions in under Gus' left hand. Gus is rigid, because with the angle he cannot see his hand. But, he hears the stove turn on.

"Now Gus…You loss 25 million pounds…"

"I know!" He shouts in protest as his fear has his face quaking as well. The slap that follows this outburst comes from Randall and splits his lip.

"Don't you dare get chippy! Now as I was saying you loss the currency so I have been pondering how much each digit should be worth. Five million pounds per would leave you useless to me, but a reminder is needed. So I figured ten million per knuckle, which means a whole pinky and a half finger should suffice. You will remember every time you tie your loafers, tying a tie and even dancing with your cheap lasses. So tighten up Butter Cup."

The first cut happens so quickly that Gus can just inhale. Second cut he just groans as his pinkie is forever lost as he hears the bone tap against the tea cup. The last cut brings a shout as she needs three tries to get through the thickness of swollen bare knuckle boxing fourth finger. As the

digit falls away the guard squeezes him tighter.

"Now that was the easy part. Here comes the pain."

Dolores says far away as he is slipping into unconsciousness.

However, he is jerked back as she rams the red hot flat iron

on the bleeding stump that was his pinky. The smell of flesh

and blood cooking causes his innards to froth into his throat,

but he chokes it back. As the irons peels back the cool air

gives him some relief than the second burn happens. This

time it's a thimble he thinks as the heat circles the entire

finger. It pulls away and he drops into his seat and squeezes

the pain radiating up his arm.

"Now Gus. Get out of here and don't even think

about irritating the situation with the Cashmeres. That will

be my option at a later date. Now bag those bloody things

and place them in the freezer. I will grind them up later and

feed them to Archibald."

Aghast, Gus trembles as he grabs his fingers and looks forlorn. After this he has to put up with his own fingers to be fed to a bull mastiff. The Cashmeres will pay with or without her permission.

Chapter 7

An Invitation

Being arrested for something you have not done is hurtful. Worse still being held is being questioned non-stop for hours over the same nothing is irritating. However, the most dreadful thing is being cuffed to the floor in front of a table where the chain is too short to rest your head on your hands and the table too filthy to rest your head. Cash has been in the same position for hours and he knows his son is in the same predicament. The coppers have held them and asked every feasible question about the garage "mayhem", as they say. Ownership had been verified and there are five "bodies" being recovered and identified.

Cash's concern is the garage still standing after the explosions, fire and water that put out that fire? As much as he has asked there is no definite answer. Not only is the garage condition in his mind, but the agony he is feeling as the adrenaline has worn off. His knees and back are stiff from the running and jumping. This has been made worse being chained in this half sitting up position for the last six hours. The room stinks of sweat and is cold. There are several initials and curses carved in the table before him and he has read them countless times to pass the time. Waiting for the inspectors to come back the hands on the clock slowly click away. Finally, the door swings open and here comes his lawyer finally. In walks his attorney, Shamus Cashmere, his often late and inconsistent cousin. Behind him comes Inspectors Glass and Thomas and neither look happy to see Shamus.

"Alright, get the shackles off of my client!" Shamus bellows with a flourish of his right meaty hand adorned with a massive gold ring. Shamus is late and inconsistent, but he is a great attorney. His practice flourishes on the side of the law in family matters, namely divorces. Divorces not in the common sort, but high profile and wealthy clientele. Bailing his cousins out is just a family responsibility. He does not have the Cashmere pension for baldness, but he loves the

rugged dreadlocks in a tapered finish on the edges. Him

being a giant of a man gives pause too many a hostile

husbands and bitter wives who end up on opposite side of

the aisle.

Inspector Thomas unlocks the manacles with a little

too much pressure on the wrist. This Inspector with his red

hair and freckles remind him of the ugly cover character in

the MAD magazines he read as a boy. When freed Cash rubs

both wrists and stands up to stretch his aching back.

"So Inspector, would you like to tell him the news? I

have no problem doing it."

As Inspector Glass runs his fingers through his raven

hair and mumbles something. Shamus just steps to Cash's

side and grabs him by the elbow as they head for the door.

They both push past and head out of the door, Ronald is

already waiting in the hallway. He too looks bedraggled and

frustrated.

"Good you both are here and I only have to say this once." He starts with the audience of inspectors and the Cashmeres fully attentive.

"First, all potential charges are dropped since they have identified the hooligans as repeat offenders. This was also supported by the video evidence of the robbery at the bank. Now on the case of the currency there was approximately 30 million pounds stolen and all of that cannot be accounted for due to fire and explosions. That is the good news." Shamus says and the inspectors and the cops move to different areas of the station before the bad news comes.

"So that means we're good then?" Ronald asks in a hopeful voice.

Cash on the other hand leans his frame against the wall as if bracing for a blow to his body. He inhales and signs his finger in a circular motion to cue Shamus to keep going.

"Now the bad news is that out of the five levels of the garage, the middle three were not damaged by fire. But, all five floors were heavily damaged by explosion and subsequent structural damage when the garage split on the last explosion. The garage is a total loss. Sorry, Ronald. We will have to review the insurance papers for getting the garage back up and running."

Young Ronald places his hand on the back of his father's neck as the older man moans in pain. The bitterness and injustice of what has transpired magnifies as looks and sees on the television that his 200 hundred pound gambling note is a loser as it floats from the hole in his pocket. As he straightens up the light in his eyes has dimmed a little bit.

They both follow Shamus to the front where they can grab their belongings that were confiscated. After grabbing their stuff, they all step outside and exchange family pleasantries. Shamus' Mother who was sister to Cash's mother still cooked dinner on Sundays, where an invitation was relayed to father and son.

"Come on gents, let's go. I am parked right over here." Shamus says and directs them to a shiny red BMW. They all pile in and drive back towards Shore ditch. While riding they listen to the radio and just decompress and absorb all of the day's events.

"Cousin Shamus. Would you mind going by the garage first? Pop and I have our vehicles there." Ronald asks from the backseat. Without an answer, Shamus signals to the left and heads toward the East End.

"Ronald, how much insurance did you have?"

"Not enough to rebuild, but maybe enough to pay the customers that cars were destroyed. I had to drop the coverage due to the flow of traffic has gone down, due to the new rail line being opened."

Rounding the corner, everyone inhales as the sight of yellow tape and water drain from the garage. Since it is now night time it seems more ominous as the garage looks like a toppled glacier. There are no lights in the garage since the

54

power is out. They all step out of the sedan and just stare at

the destruction. Handshakes all around and Shamus heads

off into the night. Father and son head into the garage to see

if they can get their vehicles out.

They both enter the garage and smell the noxious

order of smoke damage. Using their cellphone lights they

find their way to the vehicles. Cash opens the trunk and

hands his son an electric torch and they survey the damage.

"Let's stay down here, Pop. We can look at the rest in

the morning."

"Sure."

They head back towards the stairs and see the rivulets

of water still flowing down the steps. Not wanting to go up

they turn back towards the ramp, but both stop as they see

the booth door swinging open. As they walk towards the

booth there is a crash behind them. They both whip around

and see chunks of cement fall from the upper section of the

ramp. Their nerves still being on edge, they both exhale and turn back around. However, the booth is now closed. While still moving forward they split away from the door just in case there is someone waiting to ambush them from earlier. When they reach the booth they both see the cloth bag sitting on the desk next to the toppled television. Ronald opens the door and pokes the bag with his torch.

"Don't do that!" Cash hisses.

Ronald shrugs his shoulders and looks at his father like what else can happen. He smiles at his father and pokes it again with a smile. His father looks at him more sternly so he does it again and it falls open. Both smiles turn to open mouths as a diamond and a ruby rattle to the floor. Squeezing into the booth together they grab the bag and open it displaying ten gems the size of cumquats.

"Are they real?" Ronald whispers while he is looking around.

Cash takes out a diamond and slides it down the glass and it cuts the glass with no pressure.

"Yes" Cash answers and drops it back in the bag.

"Are we being set up and reaches for his gun while he looking around."

"I don't think so. Who would...?" Cash starts to say then he sees the envelope.

While they are both mesmerized there was an envelope under the bag they did not see addressed to Pearl Security Consultants with an address. As they read the address, they both turn and see the address on the building across the street.

Chapter 8

The Line in the Sand

Ool had studied and watched the two men across the street for weeks. Pondering how to approach and making sure his offer was right. It took him and the crew exactly three rotations around their home star, which equaled to Earth's three months. The entire journey here, he continued to gather data from stray data streams that float through the galaxy. Data inclusions were of news from the planet, games that were played with hard shells on their heads and great turmoil of the landscape of the planet. Gleaning information in that capacity he began to understand their financial systems and so many differences between the classes. They were ones that had much wealth and others that struggled to survive in vast wastelands such as it is on Orenthia.

His ship's crew went through their ship board duties, but also prepared the equipment to be presented for appraisal for tonight's meeting. As they entered the galaxy more information was more direct such as the physiology limitations and needs for this species. Drilling through this data gave them the forethought to think ahead. Ool bounced around in his cabin between the sleep in the chamber to recharging tank just to keep his mind awake. This mission is far beyond the scope of what he dreamed three and half cycles before. The freedom of his planet is now being negotiated by a mid-level facilitator.

Besides the pilot he did bring two creators of weaponry and equipment from the Scientific Wing, Laz and Prill. They both designed the current weapons that the Orethians chased him through the city trying to kill him. It is different on each planet where weapons are used. The projectile weapons on earth use a powder when ignited cause an explosion and the force directs the projectile at a target. This is due to the atmospheric make-up that has oxygen. It continues to cross into weapons on a larger scale as well. Zinghavi does have the necessary percentage of oxygen to ignite such a weapon, however too much oxygen. This is what Prill explained in agonizing fashion!

Prill is not the typical Zinghavian in the terms of height as he is at least a head and a half taller than most. His feather and plumage pattern is brighter than the blues of his own coat. So in turn with these bright feathers he wears tunics with deep openings in the front and no sleeves. Quite the preener he is. Listening to his speeches with the floating holo displays and the hint of lizard eggs on his breath. He wished he could shoot him with the gun he kept describing how it worked.

Prill and Laz designs used propellant charged ammunition with propellant charged launchers. Imitating the visuals from the collected data the weapons are similar to Earth's. They will work on the gravity fields on Zinghavi. Prill with his knowledge of the Orethian anatomy took pleasure in finally designing weaponry to end his previous customers. Also, the combination of Earth explosive types and merging them with their weaknesses kept him whistling the Subterranean Harmonic Tunnels Anthem. Catchy enough they all hummed along throughout the day.

As he looks at the room he sees the room is artfully decorated with leathers and dark woods. The flat is the place he rented from the gentleman "online" and it was fully furnished. Processing the gems to cash was a little harder, but he was successful in that endeavor as well. There is a knock at the door...

"Pop are you sure about this? A bag of jewels and a note and here we are?" Ronald says as he and his father ringing the buildings ringer. It is late and no one is on the street and that gets his hackles raised even higher.

"Look Son. The garage is finished and we are at the bottom. How much worse can this be? Let's see what they

61

have to say. Anything sketchy we still have these." He says as he lifts the back of his tattered uniform shirt.

"Pop. These many jewels they are guaranteed to have more weapons than these hand cannons. But, wherever you go, I go." Ronald rubs his hands over his face and pumps his arms readying himself for a fight.

After the ringing stops there is a click as the door is released. The duo look at each other and shoulder their way through the door. The building has been redone recently as their boots squeak across the new tile. Heading for the stairs they climb the up to flat number three through a nicely lit archways starting at each level. There is a smell of new woodwork in the air.

"Pop, this is a nice place. I don't remember any work crews being here to do all of this work? Do you?"

"No. I was just thinking of the same thing."

They continue to make the climb and there is only the click of the gems in the bag. As they breathe, their cavalier behavior recedes and the realization of a possible trap is on both their minds. Stepping onto the third floor there is a blind man sitting with his dead eyes in a three piece suit. His eyes have the cloudiness of advanced glaucoma, but the suit is Brooks Brothers. He is pristine in his appearance and he is not familiar.

"Evening, Mr. Cashmere and son. I am Harold and I am here to greet you with tonight's instructions." He says in a West Indian lilt. His skin is the color of burnished mahogany and his hair is silver with curly texture. He stands up and towers of them.

"Evening, Harold." Ronald says and places himself between Harold and his father.

"There is no need to be nervous young Ronald. I am not here to hurt anyone."

They look at each other perplexed.

"Oh, I am blind indeed. However, Ronald you outweigh your father by at least 30 kilos and the floor squeak told me you came closer."

"Wow, Harold. You are more astute than I gave you credit for. Since I see that you are quite aware, can I ask you a question?" Cash asks. He squares up and shifts his weight to his right and Harold keens his ear in his direction.

"Ask your question, but do not test me. I heard you shift just to check again. You ask your question and I will allow you in for this introductory meeting."

"Who are we dealing with?" Ronald asks before Cash can ask. This abrupt infraction earns a smack to the back of the head. Sheepishly he allows his father to lead.

"Never mind. Harold would you please?" Cash says. Cash strokes his goatee absently as he waits for the issue he and Ronald will have to contend with. They always have the choice to walk away, but do they get to keep the jewels?

"Cashmeres this is a one choice opportunity. The choice is to walk away right now with the jewels you have right now. They will bring you a sum that neither of you will have to work again. In reference to that retreat there will be no further contact from "our" benefactor. This parcel of jewels you have is to wet your beak as they say." Harold further emphasizes the offer by gesturing to the stairway. Just a few seconds in his pause he cocks his head to and fro not hearing any movement.

"Pop. Are we going to do this?" He asks as the bag of gems start to feel real heavy in his hands. His close shorn head is beaded in sweat as the possibility of millions already in his possession.

"Ronald. You have the choice to walk away, but I am too curious to let this go. Who would leave that much money without a worry? We could have just taken the sack and ran. Tore up the address and be out of the country by morning. I am tired of scraping and beating ourselves." Cash moves in front of his son.

"Go on. What happens now?"

Harold smiles broadly as he pulls his hand back and straightens his tie.

"Gentlemen. You walk into this door and your life is going to change. This is no criminal you will be dealing with, but a visionary on a mission to change a world. In a sign of trust place your heaters in this lock box with the gems. They will be held by me since this meeting is set for just you, the owners of Pearl Security Consultants. Have an open mind and be prepared to have your limits pushed." Harold points to the lockbox with two keys and waits.

Cash and Ronald place their weapons in the box with the gems. The box is velvet lined and they each get a key. At this point being this close to Harold they see the scars and swollen joints of a past brawler. He smells of spice and soap. Dressing a bull up as gentleman. His ear twitches as they locked their box and stepped back. There was no ear piece

and from what they could see no cameras. Both looked at

each other and nod.

"We are ready, Sir" they say in unison.

Harold smiles broadly and grabs the door knob with

no searching or hesitation. The door opens wide without a

sound and soft light pours out of the room. They both enter

the space on tentative feet as their eyes adjust to the softer

light in the room. Once in, Harold closes the door softly

behind them with a click. They are in a sitting room that is

well-appointed and see the sofas, which truly looked inviting.

"Not on your life. They look comfortable, but they will

have the drop on us if we can't get up." Instead he points to

the right where there is a wooden table with hard chairs. As

he looks around the edges of the room are in deep shadow

and sees different shades in those shadows. His father notes

the same thing and tilts his eyes to the same spot. They both

head to the table and sit and wait.

The floors are covered in carpet and their steps are muffled. Lights in the room come from overhead can lights turned off in certain areas to enhance the shadows. The atmosphere in the room has a different smell that is hard to place.

"Ronald do you remember that Indian restaurant in Piccadilly? They use that spice that is so robust, this room smells similar."

"Cardamom. It's called cardamom and it does smell like that in here."

"Well, we like the smell of it. It soothes our senses in this place." A voice says in front of them and they both jump at the voice that is too loud and choppy. They both jump from their chairs to put a barrier between them and the voice. As their hearts race there is another shift to the left of the table, where a bottle of Blanton's Straight from the Barrel whiskey is lit by an overhead light with two glasses and a bin of ice. Along with the set- up there are two ear pieces.

"Put those in so we can talk. Your language I have not learned too good yet. " The overly loud voice instructs from the shadows. Both of them grab the ear pieces that resemble Bluetooth hands free devices. After hooking them into their ears a voice introduces himself...

"I am Ool and I would like to do business with you."

Chapter 9

The Proposal

The audacity of this statement blows Cash away. As he sits and looks to his right and sees his son with the same incredulous face. His answer to this question is grabbing the two glasses and placing two cubes of ice in each. Looking to his son he holds up three fingers and Cash pours both of them three fingers. As the sip and admire the slow burn and smoothness they remain silent. After a few beats and another sip Cash finally answers.

"Sir. I understand what you are asking, but you are not an English gentlemen. How can you lay that statement out and I don't know you?"

"I agree with my Pop. Harold is a cool fella, but this is so off. We can't see you, but you have us surrounded. We walk in without weapons and with trust. So you have to show yourself or thank you for the drinks."

There is shuffling behind them and the sounds are moving away. The can lights behind them begin to light up and the room is decorated with exquisite art pieces. As the men sip they continue to glance around and see that the room is cleared. However, the area in front of them remains dark.

"I apologize for...manners. You are correct that I am not British. Also, my name is Ool."

Cash mouths the name and Ronald looks bewildered by the name as well. They both drain the rest of their glass and pour another.

"Okay, Mr. Ool. Where are you from? What can we do for you?"

"Mr. Cashmere...I am not from here and for us to get acquainted. Now if I show you who I am and what I am, you must give me an opportunity to understand what the proposal is. Do I have your word as gentleman?"

Both men look at each other and both say, "Yes."

The lights behind the table turn up fully and both men choke and jump up from the table. Both men stare at their glasses and then at each other to verify they are not hallucinating. Their boots squeak as they back up and see Mr. Ool. He standing and is at least 5'11", but the sights that have them bewildered are the feathers. The "man" is covered in feathers colored blue and green. He is also wearing a shirt down to his "waist" with a kilt! But, the final straw are the eyes shaped like ice cream cones and follow each of them separately. The silence in the room lasts a long time. Ool watches the two men as they continue you to stoop over, walk around the room and stare at him then repeat the process. After this happens for the next fifteen minutes they sit back down.

Cash places both his elbows on the table and covers his face. Ronald sits back in his seat and stares at the ceiling.

"I hope this is a joke and someone jumps out with a camera." Cash mumbles behind his hands.

Ool laughs to himself and pours himself a drink as well. Over the last couple of cycles he has grown to like this Earth beverage. He takes a long pull and leans back in his seat as well.

"No there are no cameras and I am in dire need of your services. I have come a long way to talk to you."

"Why us? What kind of help do you need? We own what is left of a parking garage." Ronald says as he continues to stare at the ceiling.

"My planet is in trouble and we need a group of people to get us free. We are not fighters so we made a partnership with a different race name the Orethians. This partnership has now turned to us being infiltrated by them. So we need the Pearl Services to get us free."

The incredulous looks on both men's faces turn into laughter. As they are laughing they look at him and realize he is not joking.

"How did you find us?" Cash says as he gets his laughter under control.

"I found your name under Security in the words after a movie called the Magnificent Sven."

"Do you mean seven?"

"No, Sven. Certain words in your language don't translate to ours so it may sound jumbled or dumb." The other word with St and p is another one."

"Well I understand and my father had that contract years ago. The company has…"

After finishing his drink, Ool answers.

"The company failed not because of you, but your brother and his vices. I researched that from the signals on the ship on the trip here."

Ronald strokes his chin and asks the question that neither have asked.

"Why are you asking us? Have you contacted the British government or better yet the Yanks? This is more of their speed saving countries and saving a planet is only a step up?"

"If you don't care, can we move to the comfort seats over there?"

All three get up and they both look and see that Ool is short. They watch him waddle to leather seat with the ottoman. Ronald grabs the bottle and the both take their glasses with them. They sit next to each other on the sofa and get comfortable.

"The reason I am not contacting the government, because they will want to cut me up and study me first. You have seen the July 4th movie. Second, we are entrenched with the problems with the Orethians. Just imagine what will happen if I let them on my planet? They will just try to rob us and the politicians will get it all. I watched the elections between the men with the big hair in America. Lastly, smaller is better for more precision."

"Those are all valid points. The question still has not been answered, what do you want us to do?" Cash asks as he looks at his watch.

"We want you to exterminate them and chase them off our world." Ool says with a coldness that surprises them.

"Mr. Ool that is dark. So let me understand you want my son and I to get rid of them. This is not a movie! You want us to go to outer space and kill people that used to work with you?"

"Yes. We are the good guys and they are the bad guys. White hats versus black hats." Ool says and pours another drink.

"What you are asking is more in a gray area, Sir. How do we know that you just want us to kill a competitor or suppress a "race"? You have to show us more than a bag of gems."

"I agree with my Pops. I served this country and gray work is a lot more complicated."

Ool understands and stands to his feet. He gestures for them to stand up as well.

"Well I will show you. This will convince you, but let us do this in the morning. You gentlemen are tired and you need to be well rested for what I have to show you."

Everyone gives their salutations and the two men head towards the door. Once the door opens, Harold is standing to the left of the door with their case in his hands.

"Harold, will help you process the invitation fee and let you know the address of the next meeting." Ool says and closes the door behind them.

Harold continues to stand there with a smile on his face.

"Harold, what does he mean "invitation fee"?" Ronald asks as he looks back at the door.

"Mr. Cashmere, the bag in this box was just for you just to have this initial conversation. Before, you ask I can't see, so I don't know what Mr. Ool looks like. But, I know he pays me well and I will continue to protect this relationship. And yes I know they are not from here, however the money is green."

No one can argue with the man's assessment so they both unlock the box and grab their belongings. Looking at his watch Cash realizes it is 3 am and he is exhausted. They both turn to walk away. However, Ronald turns around to ask a question.

"What did he mean you can help us with the fee?"

"You cannot deposit those gems in the bank. Converting them into currency is a job I can do for you. You have to set up an offshore account to send the money. The key is that it will be a lot of money and such an influx of cash will have questions raised."

"You can do that? This is not a pig in poke, eh?" Ronald says skeptically. Always on guard for a hustle keeps him wary and alive.

"Definitely not a pig in a poke. Yes, I was not always blind you know. I worked in finance in the West Indies before the accident. Set the account up and I suggest the Caymans or Bahamas. Less questions than Switzerland. Have a good morning." Harold says and walks past both of them and heads down the stairs with no hesitation.

Chapter 10

A Message

"No one is here right now." The hoodie says in the cellphone.

"Good. You take the guys and sweep that garage and make sure there is no money left in there. I want every loose pound gathered and set the charges to level the rest of the garage." Gus growls in the phone. His hand will not stop throbbing and that continues to stoke his anger.

"Understand. Wait, here they come." The hoodie says and keeps walking past the garage.

"Do they see you?"

"No. They are talking and going in the garage."

"Watch them! They may be going back to look for the money as well!" Gus screams in the phone.

The hoodie makes a left and crosses the street to see if they come out. As he gets even with the garage headlights are headed out and a second car as well. Both men are driving their own vehicles.

"Looks like they just came to get their cars, Gus."

"Get to what I told you to do. Set the charges for 6 am." Gus says and ends the conversation.

The group of ten men scour the garage and spot a bag in a pile of rubble under the ramp. Gathering all the wet, loose and burned notes amount to another half a bag. While the gathering has been going on the other half of the crew set charges on every remaining pillar to level the structure. All the timers are set and they all leave.

These type of activities are not without notice. Ool watches from across the street and understands that this act pushes them closer to helping him, so he does nothing. Ool and the ship's crew head out of the building through the back entrance where their transport waits. They have to get back to the ship to charge then prepare for the Cashmeres request.

In the still of the morning and the only witnesses to see the destruction of the garage are the stray cats in the rubbish bin across the street. The explosions are deafening and the entire block wakes to the shaking and rumbling of the five level garage cascading to the ground. It takes out the cars in the surrounding lots and the building across the street as the expanse of concrete acts like a juggernaut leaving dust and a chorus of car alarms and shattered windows. In the end it will be classified as a gas leak explosion in weakened lines, hence freeing the Cashmeres of responsibility. Much to the chagrin of Gus.

Chapter 11

Heads or Tails

Meanwhile in Shoreditch, father and son are eating breakfast in the kitchen of the family row house. The home has been in the family since Cash's grandfather bought it when Shoreditch was a better section of the city. This property just like the garage is the last of the family's assets. Sitting at the table over a breakfast of sausage, eggs and muffins there is banter back and forth over yesterday's activities.

"Pop, all this has happened in a day! We get in a gunfight, garage gets wrecked and we meet an alien."

"I know. What will happen today?" He answers back with a laugh.

The bag of gems sits between both of them and they continue to poke it to make sure they were not dreaming.

"So the first order of business is to get to the garage and clear out the cars. Then open that account Harold suggested. Still can't believe it."

Ronald pours himself another cup of coffee and takes a bite of eggs.

"Now Pop. The money will be ours and we can say, no. I am having a hard time thinking about going to play a copper in outer space. This is so outrageous!"

"Yes it is. Remember what I always taught you. One foot in front of the other. We will figure it out, but for now control what we can control."

"So do we tell anyone?"

"Not right now. We handle the small stuff first then we wait."

There is a pounding on the front door and they both look at each other shocked. Cash waves to Ronald to hide the bag. They had both showered and were in casual clothes to just be in the house, tee shirts and lounge pants. Cash slides on his slippers and heads to the front door, as Ronald places the gems in the chiller behind the food. The pounding continues.

"I am coming. Hold on!"

As he opens the door, Shamus barges in. Looking a little bit disheveled wearing a sweat suit and slippers with his hair all tousled.

"What is it? Why are you so agitated?"

"The garage is gone."

"What do you mean gone? We were just there early morning."

"Gas line blew and leveled the whole thing."

Cash is rocked back on his heels. He knew in his heart he would get it fixed and now totally gone.

"When did this happen?" Ronald says as enters the room wiping his hands off from the ice.

"The coppers say at 6. You two were here right?"

"Yes of course. Don't tell me the coppers want us for this?"

"Well, no. Not yet." Shamus stammers and pushes past both of them and heads to the kitchen. He grabs a glass and heads for the chiller. Both men freeze and watch him open the freezer and grab some ice then pour some orange juice. They both release a held breath.

"Okay. We were here if the Inspectors call."

Shamus drains the juice and places the glass in the sink.

"Okay. I tried to call both of you. Where are your phones?"

"Upstairs. We were having breakfast and planning for the day."

"Scratch number one off of the list." Ronald mumbles.

Shamus shakes his head and heads out of the front door to his car. With a squeal of tires he heads off to home.

Cash closes the door and they head back to the kitchen.

There is silence as the news has sunk in.

"So what are we going to do? The garage is gone so we have nothing else."

"Son, I have to say this could be a great sign for something better. How would you do it? If we went through with this with Ool. That is a bizarre name."

"For a bizarre alien. Pop, I can't answer that until we understand it all. It's easy to fight for Queen and country, but mercenary work is about the cause and the payoff."

"So if we do it. It has to be all in or all out. If we cash in the gems we are in, period."

As they both look at the freezer.

"How much money do you have on you Pop?"

"Three hundred pounds and another thousand in the bank, why?"

"I have a thousand upstairs and another two thousand quid in the bank. We can wait to cash those in. I need to know more. Remember, owe no man or Ool." He says with a laugh and his father joins in with them as they toast glasses. After they clean up the breakfast dishes they head to their floors to get things done for the day. The Cashmere home was set up that Cash has the second floor and Ronald the third.

Cash lays out his clothes for the day on his side of the bed. He never touches his wife's side of the bed. Arial Cashmere is and was the love of his life. Even when things got bad she always comforted him in those situations. When Ronald was with the 1 Assault Group Royal Marines, she and he would keep daily prayer vigils for Ronald. Ronald was their only child due to complications, but he was more than boy enough for them. As he goes to the closet where her clothes still hang, he grabs a satchel for the day's activities.

Upstairs Ronald is booting up his laptop and while he waits checks his phone. Shamus did call four times. Ronald still kept his room in good order since his stint in the Royal

Marines. Sometimes to be honest he missed it and his brothers. They are still his only brothers as he is an only child. His life has been great with the best parents. This is why he still lived at home, because of his Pop. Losing Mom to cancer always ground in his gut. Sitting in Afghanistan he never knew, because they wanted him to keep his mind on his job. By the time he got back she only had months left. Those months he wished they were years. He did everything he could to make sure was okay. But, she made him promise to take care of his Pops, no matter what. This he would do till he died, which would leave him an orphan. He jumps up and cranks out fifty push-ups to chase away the darkness with adrenaline. As he finishes he gets up and see the laptop is ready. He searches the banks in the areas Harold suggested. No decision yet, but be ready.

After he and his father got the accounts opened and transfer a deposit they sit back and wait for the confirmation email.

"Ronald I appreciate you looking at this with me. We are partners and will continue to split everything down the middle with no secrets."

"Of course. But, can you imagine us being in a space suit bouncing around." He says and mimicking with his cheeks puffed out and swinging his arms. They both laugh. The email dings with the confirmation and then dings again from an unknown address. It reads;

40239 Rye St

West Street Borough

2:00 pm Today

Thanks,

O

They read it over and wonder what is next.

"How did he get our email address?"

"Son, it's on our business cards and the sign on the garage." Cash says with a laugh.

Ronald smacks his forehead and gets up.

"Where are you going? Getting dressed and grabbing a coin."

"Coin for what?"

"Heads or tails. But, I kind of want to do it."

"Me too. Forget the coin and get dressed. I say heads we do it or tails we do it." Cash   says as he rubs his hands together for the next adventure.

Chapter 12

How Much?

Ronald turns down Rye Drive and looks for the address. The weather as usual is misty for April and a little bit chilly. He opted for jeans, boots and a flannel shirt. His father on the other hand loves the old Englishman look, slacks, tweed vest and bowtie. They both are more curious than nervous. The area is not like the urban settings of London, it has the country feel with the vegetation with very few structures.

"Where is this address?" Ronald asks.

"The numbers don't even go that high?"

They travel another mile or two then they see their contact, Harold sitting on a bench. He is sitting there in a suit with an umbrella.

"I bet our old friend knows. Pull over and pick him up."

Ronald pulls to the side of the road and rolls down the window. There he sits with a smile.

"Knew it was you. Mr. Cashmere I was sent here to escort you the rest of the way."

"So you just assumed we were coming?"

"No assumption, I know. The possibility of what can happen to what you have now is too intriguing. I have been down that road. Now let us be off. Keep straight into the road in the marshlands exactly three miles then stop."

"You heard the gentleman, Ronald. Let us be off." Cash says with a smile. He tips his driving hat and grins, because he likes this guy.

They roll along in Ronald's Audi with the worn interior and the lingering smell of the aftershave his father always wears. That smell permeates every vehicle and couch, which is why Ronald will never get rid of this car.

"Nice car." Ronald says from the backseat.

"Audi right. I can tell from the seats and idle of the engine."

"So what are we getting today?"

"The realization of what is happening and what they want you to do."

"Oh, by the way we set up the accounts. So if this goes well we need your help to get the gems converted."

"Not an issue." He says and rolls down the window.

"Stop the car, we are here."

Ronald stops pulls over in the middle of the marshlands. In the water there is a metal pad with wooden pallets leading up to it. So they follow the path and look back and see Harold get back in the car. He sits behind the steering wheel and turns on the radio. A slow rhythm of music wafts over to them as the platform begins to go, up. The ship is cloaked and this is really getting serious. As they reach the next stopping point there is a welcoming party. They have arrived in a storage area and there is Ool with three other "Ool's"? All of them are alike, but different. They put in their earpieces and get ready for what will be a long day.

"Before we get started. Please let me make introductions. This is Prill." Ool says as he points to a taller one with bright blue feathers and open shirt.

"This is Laz." He points to a one similar in height but with red feathers.

"Lastly, this is Slill." As he points to the last one with orange feathers.

"Flock these are the Cashmeres, Ronald Jr and Ronald III. Hopefully, we can get them to help us. So let us show them what we have and so that they can evaluate if they want to assist us."

They all leave and head up a ramp to what they guess is a common room. They all sit and they prepare to cover what they need to know.

Slill begins the presentation on the history of the Zinghavi and the Orethians. He covers the war, the agreements and the destruction of the partnership. The convincement came in the videos of the public shaming and execution of Zinghavians. This reminded Ronald of the executions in Afghanistan by ISIS. At this memory the anger is reignited and the ache returns. His father noticing this places a reassuring hand on his shoulder.

Slill was followed by Laz whose information got their attention on Orethians physiology. The average height is seven foot and taller with a reptilian coat that is necessary on their desert planet. It operates as an armor, but also a shell to retain moisture. The skin is resistant to metal and high velocity ammunition will not work.

"So what has been tried if metal doesn't work?" Cash asks as he leans forward further intrigued.

"We don't know as we have never tried to kill one." Laz responds.

"Why not? I see they have no problem killing any of you. Also, are they cannibals? They bit chunks out of the one with the green feathers." Ronald says.

"Well they are not cannibals per say as in your race. But, they usually maim us to show dominance. Trying to kill them and fail would bring us more pain, so no." Ool answers.

"What is the atmosphere like on your planet? Also, what are the radiation levels in comparison to Earth?" Ronald asks as the plan is formulating in his mind.

"The Earth's atmosphere is 78% nitrogen, 21% oxygen, .9% argon and .03% carbon dioxide. Zinghavi atmosphere has higher oxygen at 23%, 73% nitrogen, 3% carbon dioxide and 5% of other inert gases. So anyone you will need regulate oxygen and standard weapons will fire, but the volatile nature would cause weapon and personal damage." Laz explains as he reviews the data on his pad.

Cash and Ronald ponder this information.

"So it would be best for us to live on a ship." Ronald says and gets up to walk around and look closer at the ship.

"Living on a ship will keep our living quarters stable and mobile. This will also help in keeping our food stores and not being able to be tracked or predictable. However, a base would be better on second thought to give us room."

They all nod in agreement. Further discussion is had and further planning on setting up a ship for those purposes.

"Understand. Let's move on." Cash says as his son seethes.

They further cover the perceived weaknesses of vision. This is where the possibility of them being blind to heat. Just this fact alone gives them the upper hand where body heat can't be seen. Zinghavians have cooler blood due to the water they hold inside to function. Heat blindness gives them such an advantage. As their minds absorb all of this, Prill starts to begin his briefing. Cash waves for him to stop.

"No disrespect Mr. Prill. We have to talk to Mr. Ool about compensation."

"We are interested, but we do not want to give away any of our ideas without a deal." Ronald adds. Prill's feathers seem to glow as he is shut down for this change of direction. Cash passes his son a bottle of water and a sandwich out of his satchel that he brought. Surprisingly they did not ask for their guns today as he moves it to the side to grab his own sandwich. As they eat Cash observes the Zinghavians before him. They are only different in their own ways not just in the color of their feathers. The weight is one factor, but he sees the difference in the mannerisms in how they carry themselves as well.

Ool is nervous with energy as he waits and watches them eat. Slill is the oldest and it is evident in his movements as he is slower and watches everyone as he sits. Prill on the other hand is confident in who he is as he continues to watch himself in the glass. He flexes and primps his chest feathers. Laz is studious and does not have confidence in who he is as he continues to watch the ground.

As they are being observed the same is being done to them by Ool. The size of the men is intimidating to him, because of the height and muscle density. They both move with confidence and their eyes miss nothing. Mr. Cashmere is older, but still fit enough to handle himself as he saw at the garage battle. His eyes, bald head and beard emit a strength and cunning that keeps his nape feathers tingling. Ronald Cashmere has the same intensity as his father, but his eyes absorb everything as well. He is more powerfully built at his age and has hair. His beard is different, but he has a more relaxed nature than his father.

Ool steps forward and waves everyone to be quiet and says some small words to Laz to assure him. He takes his seat across from the Cashmeres and prepares for negotiations.

"Mr. Cashmere and Ronald Cashmere, first I want to say thank you for coming."

"Ool call me Cash and this is Ronald. Let's keep this casual and see what you are offering."

Ool smiles and pushes a button then starts to read from his holo tablet.

"Mister...I mean Cash. I found a lot of data and did not know how to approach this. First, I looked at the military compensation and that seemed to low. The reason is I see that is because it is so many of them so the compensation is low. Next I checked the pay for business people and that was confusing as well." Ool says as he nervously fidgets trying to keep their attention. Ronald looks at his father and shakes his head.

"Ool relax. What did you come up with?" Cash asks as he dusts of his trousers and re-crosses his leg to be more relaxed.

As he takes a deep breath, he understands that he can lose them right now. His breathing becomes more labored. He places his head down before he starts to speak.

"Okay...I looked at a prestigious group the NFL player. Since this is one of the highest paid occupation, I found an average of 600,000 dollars per player. Is that fair?"

"No, Sir! We are British! Not Americans so we only have one football and that is soccer." Ronald says as he is getting exasperating with the insult. He then pulls out his phone and searches for his response. After a moment he shows his father his phone.

"Excuse my son's exuberance, but he is right. You are asking us to get into your fight and leave our planet. So the compensation for that will be higher. The average Premier Footballer is 50000 pounds per week, which is 3.7 million pounds per year."

Ool stares at him blankly as if this number does not bother him, so Cash keeps going.

"Ool this is our proposal for what we will do and what you can expect." Cash says as he pulls out an envelope from his satchel. Ool shows his hand in an upward motion for Cash to keep going. The rest of the crew focus in and giving the negotiations their full attention.

"Okay. That figure is for the individuals that will leave Earth to go to your world on two year contracts. The two years cannot be served in straight time. We cannot expect someone to be in space for twenty-four months. I think three month stretches with a month off. So that is 3.7 million pounds per year for two years that is 7.4 million pounds. That is non-negotiable if they finish the two years. In event of death you pay out, period." He looks up and they are not wavering so he forges on.

"We have to prepare a team and train them in preparation to go there and that will take money. There also will be a need to develop the weapons and armaments with the help of Laz and Prill. That money is separate operating budget and that is not part of our compensation for Pearl Security. Although, the expectation is that this is yearly. We are proposing a six year contract. This six year contract will pay the company 24 million pounds per year."

That number freezes Ool as that number seems to be quite large.

"Cash, that totals out 144 million pounds in six years. That number is too large. I will consider 72 million pounds over six years."

Cash understood this was a large number, but was curious to see how high they were willing to go. It was a gamble, but he is not deterred.

"That figure is half of what we are asking. Now the problem we have is that we cannot file taxes for our work on this planet. So we have to redevelop our businesses here or better yet branch into other venture to funnel this money. So 100 million pounds over the six year contract?"

Ool never looks at his crew, but ponders the decision on his own.

"The gems that you already possess are worth 10 million pounds, so in good faith if you accept this I will do 95 million pounds over the six years. Is this a deal?"

Both men look at each other and whisper to themselves.

"Pop, 95 million quid over six years is great, but we have not been there yet. So let's do four years at 63 million quid with our option for the last two. I am going there on the first crew, anyway."

"That has not been discussed and I like the four year better."

"Ool will you do four years at 63 million pounds with our option for the last two for 37 million pounds? Maybe we will be done before that time?"

Ool nods his head and gets up and sticks his hand out.

"You shake hands on deals like this right?

Chapter 13

Hard Work

After making the deal the rest of the details have been worked out. Cash and Ronald head back out to their vehicle where Harold sits behind the wheel listening to jazz. After reshuffling their seats, Ronald turns the car around and heads back to West Street. The ride is fairly quiet as the seriousness of what just transpired and they are millionaires. This is a feeling that neither father or son really understands nor the negotiations with all those numbers flying around.

"Now Harold now that we have gone down this rabbit hole are you ready? This is quite bonkers really. I am still thinking we are dreaming." Ronald says as they pull into West Street. He pulls to the side of the road and parks and turns the radio off. The weather outside has settled down and the rain has passed. Now that the sun is out the air has become warmer, so he cracks the windows.

"Rabbit hole indeed. This plan together is not just about the money, but it is a difference for an entire world. I can't see Ool and the others, but I overhear the conversations. Those gentlemen are scared and are in need of help." Harold says in the backseat. He fingers his tie and listens to the sounds in the area.

"So this is really happening. Harold we are going to need the help with the gems so we can start setting up things in motion." Cash says.

"Well let's gets moving and can I get a lift to the tube station? I will meet you tomorrow at the pub, The Mucky Duck in White Chapel. Bring the gems and I will handle the rest. I don't have to tell you gents how to handle this."

Ronald pulls in front of the tube station and drops Harold off and pulls back into traffic. Traffic is heavier as they get back towards the East End and this gives them plenty of time to talk. While horns blare and they trot along in traffic they continue to have conversations on what to do next.

Covering issues besides the money is the gist of the

conversation at this time. The truth of what they are doing

will not get past them and they will bring in only those they

both trust. Driving and talking allows their minds to keep

flowing to formulate a longstanding program.

"Pop I want to be on the first team to go. I know you

don't want me to, but we have to really see what it is."

"Son, I don't want to lose you, first. Second, I need

you here to get things ready. Can we make a decision on that

later? We have a more pressing problem."

"What's that?" Ronald says he enters the roundabout.

"Unfortunately we will have to leave England and take

this endeavor to the United States. England is too small and

we need space and anonymity for us to build. Especially

when we have a flush amount of cash suddenly at our

disposal. Those criminals from the shootout worked for someone, which will be an issue as well?"

Ronald does not respond as he wheels the Audi to the edge of the danger tape around the remnants of the garage. Cash looks up and is silent as well. This last remaining vestige of the previous generation of Pearl Security has died here, but the new generation of Pearl has just been established. Having this silence between them as they remember the lunches and dinners brought by a wife and mother, soccer games watched and laughs shared. The rubble remains and the dust has settled so the end is defined.

Ronald strokes his goatee and voices what he is thinking.

"Pop, a gas line did not do this. Someone did this."

"I agree. So we need to get moving so someone's assumption does not kill you or me. We are leaving as soon as possible."

"Yes, Sir. But, do you think us leaving will keep the hounds from our trail?"

"It is quite easy for the hounds to find you in your den than them trailing you in a continent?"

Ronald huffs his grudging approval and knows his father is right. As he sits there is a flicker of movement in driver's side mirror. Two hoods are heading up quickly with pipes. His eyes flick to the passenger side where two more head up the other side.

"Pop! Here they come open the door!" Ronald yells as he opens his door and slams the car in reverse and steps on the gas. The car lurches with a squeal of tires and catches all four unaware. There is a crunch as both doors make contact into the lead man on either side. The momentum of that contact throws those two into the remaining men and the front tire on his side bumps into a body part. They both launch themselves from the car as both doors spring fully forward as the hinges break off and the glasses shatter.

Ronald is the first to touch the pavement and he realizes the first man is no longer a threat. The car door has flipped him forward and his shoulder is laying at an awkward angle and unmoving. His cohort is dazed and bleeding from his mouth where apparently that the first's feet clipped him under the chin. Ronald clips his chin again with a well-placed soccer kick with his boot that snaps him back to unconsciousness. He looks over and sees his father wielding a pipe like a cricket bat as he lays into both of his assailants.

Coming to assist his father he sees the damage on this side was not as severe. One is bleeding from his leg where the corner of the car door clipped his shin which is bleeding, but no breaks. He leaves this one for his father and he attacks the second one who is trying to find a space to waylay his father in his whirling dervish attack. This hood is no older than twenty-five years old and shaved clean Caucasian man. He is short and stocky and that is to his advantage. As Ronald swings with an overhead right, the shorter man ducks under and takes his legs out. Ronald lands on his assailants back as he sprawls away to counter this attack. As they both hit the ground, Ronald refuses to wrestle in the street with this kid. So he gets to his feet and catches him coming up with a knee to head that staggers him. Following with a short left sends him to the ground unmoving.

Cash steps to his son's side with the pipe slung over his shoulder. They both pick up the unconscious man a roll him in the backseat where Cash jumps in with him. Ronald drives off into the danger tape and parks across the street in front of Ool's building. They pull the man out of the backseat and carry him into the alleyway. Cash pours his water bottle on the man's face then slaps him hard across the face. Stunned green eyes open unfocused. Before they shut again

113

another hard slap knocks more of the drowsiness away. They

pin him to the building's wall and start asking the hard

questions. There are continued slaps and punches to coax

the important things out. The most important is a name that

runs ice through their veins.

"You two blokes buggered up Dolores Savage's heist!

So Gus wants us to find out where you got her money! So

you can kill me! But, there are more of us than you all day!"

Hood screams in their faces as blood spittle flies in their

faces. So with a final punch they leave him unaware and

unconscious in the alleyway.

"The United States sounds really good right now."

Cash says as he and Ronald cross to the Audi. He straightens

his vest and dusts off his trousers as they have the

justification to move their new business venture.

Part 2

Chapter 14

Assumptions

Dolores Savage being raised as the youngest child to the Opium King, she was not coddled or cajoled into believing she deserved anything. A name is a name, but the reputation and the fear associated with that name is the sum of what your lot is in life. Another thing that Ricard Savage did not tolerate was disobedience. She to this day always wore the long skirts not out of modesty, but as camouflage for her youthful expressions of that irritant. Coming to the waterfront always wreaked havoc with her raven tresses. As she stands here pondering what the next step should be, her eyes do observe the duffels sitting outside of her Navigator. Her eyes flick fiercely to her right as a groan escapes her "captive" audience. Gus and his hoodie crew are all here trussed up in the bay of the warehouse, waiting. The scene is not without its merits for her point to be understood. Gus and five of his crew are tied to chairs hands and feet bound facing each other. Each one beaten and drugged for this little gathering.

Dolores takes her time and sits at the table and chair that has been set up for her comfort. She is quite young, but her reputation has placed her in the role of the "Boss" where her superiors have no issue in taking a subservient role. Randall her most trusted assistant pours her tea into her metal cup. He came from India with regards from her father years ago. Built like a gymnast and the quickness of one while issuing violence with his whip sword keeps peace in her privacy. His long hair is tucked inside his shirt as he leaves to slap awake the last sleeper.

Gus struggles against his bonds and sees that his number two is tied up across from him. He turns his head with the queasiness' that almost causes him to lose his internal composure. While he waits for the room to settle he sees the squad he sent to relay a message to the Cashmeres. His insides turn absolutely frigid, because Randall smirks in his direction as he wipes his bloody palm on the hood of Percy. As he tries to recall what happened he hears the click of heels to his right. When he turns he sees the grim face of his end.

"Now Gus. Wake up Gus." Dolores says with a nod. Gus is slapped hard against his cheek from the precise hand of Randall. Blood exits his nose and mouth with and incisor to the hood of the man next to him. He fights the nausea and looks back at her with fear and hatred. The smell of mustiness and the echoes around him lets him know he is in a warehouse.

"So now that I have your attention. I am not asking any questions, because I know the answers. To make it up to me you went back and got the money, right?" She flicks her eyes to a barrel in the middle of the restrained employees. Both bags are tossed in there, doused with gasoline and lit. The area is engulfed with smoke and Dolores goes back to her seat as she waits for the fire to finish its work. After the flames have died down, a fire extinguisher finishes the rest. She dabs her mouth after a final sip and heads back over to continue.

"See you twit! It is and will never be about the money!" She screams and everyone bows their head as if being scolded. She regains her composure and runs her hands over her skirt to smooth out imaginary wrinkles. Even in this dark endeavor she continues to be flawless in long navy blue skirt and grey loose fitting blouse. Now that she pulled herself together. She makes an orbit around all of them.

"Now since the money is out of the way. Who was the genius who decided to level the garage? That was quite genius, but the issue is the collateral damage caused by that. Now we have coppers and investigators backtracking to who committed the crime. So where does that path lead and who is being followed? Also, now the two men that got caught in the middle are in the wind. So now those two have to be wrapped up, because one of you talked."

Without any signal or word each man has a man standing behind them. The hoodies in the chair start to look back and forth wondering what is going to happen. Randall is standing behind Gus.

"Ma'am. I miscalculated what you wanted. I thought the punishment of losing my appendage was trying to spur me to action." Gus says weakly. His loyalty is to him and his main purpose is to get from under the homicidal hands of Randall. There is a crack and he turns his head forward as his number two guy's head is laying at an awkward angle. The man who did it has a solemn face as this was his cousin.

There is the obnoxious smell of urine as one of the hoodies starts crying and he is dispatched.

"Gus I am so sorry. In this timeframe in your present, because I am unsure if you have a future as of yet. My instructions and thoughts are black and white. No means no and don't mess with the Cashmeres is clear."

"Leave them alone." He says meekly as he sees the pinkie was an easy loss. Rather quickly three more men die; one by gunshot to the back of the head, another with his throat cut and the last and the worse straggled. Gus and Percy are the last remaining while brain synapses fire last twitches and movements in their executed brethren. All men back away and drag the bodies with them. Gus and Percy are turned to face each other.

The entire exchange took less than five minutes. Dolores looks benignly at the carnage and wraps her hair in a top knot and puts on black latex gloves. Randall places another apron on his mistress. A groan comes from Percy as he sees the glove and looks around and sees the bleakness of this moment. Dolores has finished her preparations and looks at both of them for her decision. This pause in judgement has an icicle feel to the innards of both men. Suddenly with the grace of a ballerina while she pivots quickly towards Percy. Her hair whips in behind her as she closes in on Percy in two quick strides. She is not a tall woman, but there is an underlying power in her form and movements.

"Percival, please explain to me what happened this morning? I am curious on your knocks and what answers came from those knocks?"

Percy blanches at the answer he will have to give. He woke up in the alleyway with his captors picking him up and throwing him in a van. The possibilities end in the same way; either quick or long, death. She is not pacing, but is staring at him not blinking. Her hands are not visible and that causes

121

his eyes to shift from her gaze. Focusing and trying to see her

hands has him so entranced that he does not hear her clear

her throat the first time. The second one with a slap from the

man behind him brings him back. Gus watches with the

clutch of fear and acceptance.

"Well Ma'am those blokes got the jump on us. We

were just going to rough them up. They...We got beat

Ma'am."

"Percival that is not an answer. Your chaps who just

left said the same thing. I asked what you said. They were on

the street beat bloody. You however were in the alley,

worked over a little bit harder. When hard pressure is

applied hard answers are found."

After a swallow, Percy starts to cry. The crying leads

to a rambling recollection of what was done to him and what

he said. These ramblings ended while he looked Gus in the

eye before his life is winked out.

"Gus, please take care of me Mum?" Percy groans out. The anticipation of his impending death has ended his sobs and is replaced by a resolve. There is a snap and Gus' right hand is freed and he is slid next to Percy where he takes his hand pats him on the cheek with reassurance.

"So Gus. This is your mess and you need to put in the finisher. We have cleaned up the rest." Dolores says with a spin and with a flourish. She snaps her fingers and there is a blade in the hand of one of her men.

"Percival you will be leaving us now. Gus you are a knife fighter right? I would never be daft enough to give you a gun, but here is a knife to send our loose lipped associate on his way."

There are two quick swipes, one to the femoral artery and the last to the carotid artery. The life of Percival Ellis Duggan ends with a whimper and a gasp. Gus doesn't even care when she clips the fourth finger next to the scabbed stump of his pinkie. His soul has been rent as he sees the carnage of what his decision has brought on his life. Plastic is rolled out and bodies are cut loose. The men he once commanded are wrapped away as trash and he sits with blood dripping from both hands. He will not cry, but in his heart revenge will be his.

Randall collects all of Dolores' materials and loads her into the vehicle. She doesn't even look back to admire her orchestrated destruction. In truth she is the smartest one of them all, she just cut off my fingers. All the bodies are on us and she never utters an order, but just looks. Somehow he will kill her or bury her under the countless bodies sprinkled throughout London and the countryside. As she rolls through the warehouse door the smell of salt in the air clears his sinuses of all the blood he is surrounded by. Bodies meander around him as the bodies are moved to the vans to be disposed of at other locations. Gus is finally untied and given a bandage for his bleeding hand. In his mind he is trying to

decide who he hates more, Dolores or the Cashmeres.

Chapter 15

Packing Bags

After the fight with the hoodies and getting the name who is after them, they decide to stay low key. The Mucky Duck on White Chapel is not a high profile place and is relatively off the beaten path. Everyone now wants a hookah bar or vape lounge. What is wrong with having a pint and yelling at a match? Ronald and Cash arrive and find a high top up front. Sitting in the back always calls attention so sitting up front will be normal. Ronald opts for jeans and a black hoodie to hide his face with black Timberlands. As for Cash he opts for trousers and a long sleeve t-shirt with Kenneth Cole chukkas.

The pub is not that crowded with the time being after supper. The Duck has curtains to cover the lower part of the window where a person can still see the street. Harold is coming down the street and they watch around him to make sure he is not being followed. He makes the crossing with the assistance of a walking can. They are both surprised that he is even using one. He finally makes his way into the pub and Ronald calls him. He turns their direction and orders himself a water.

"Now gentlemen I have moved some money into your account. The remaining will be a reoccurring transfer monthly from three dummy corporations. I was able to obtain 80% value of the jewels, which paid you 8.5 million dollars. There is 4.5 million dollars in your accounts. The remaining four million will be transferred into your account at an amount of 333,333.00 per month."

"Harold why is it in American dollars not the Crown's pounds?" Ronald asks as he takes a look around the pub and looking up the street. He is being ever vigilant after the last few days.

"Ronald, England is only so big and London is even smaller. This sum of quid just being heard of on the streets, will have every criminal, copper and taxation representatives beating down your door. America has enough crime and issues that a few gems doesn't even raise the blood pressure of middle rung players." He says all this with a smile. Tipping his glass he takes a small sip.

"Cash what is your plan from this point? There have been some rumblings about a lot of beatings handed out on the East End. I speculate that those beatings have a familial issue to them." Harold says with a wink. The room starts to fill with the working class making a stop prior to heading home. Having a drink after work is a reward for making through a day with its issues and complaints. It is also a reinforcement for what lays for problems that lay in wait for their return. There are attorneys, construction workers and coppers sharing a pint next to each other and conversations ranging from futbol to politics.

"Well Harold. I think you have the right idea. America is quite large and a couple of gents like us would fit right in. My son and I discussed that this morning after our disagreement."

"Well let me know where you two land. I will follow behind you after that." Harold says as his ears perk up to all the conversations continue to pepper them from all angles. His head stops mid turn and he signals for them to get up and leave.

Cash and Ronald tense up and both look around. Looking to their right they see the problem and hustle Harold to the door. Pub fights start over the smallest things and this one is another man's wife has been caught with another man. The husband is now screaming and wading through the fleeing crowd with a pipe wrench. They all leave the pub and make their way down the street with their collars and hoods pulled up. Their walking and discussions center on what is next.

"Harold, why in the world would you want to come with us? You surely have the money and connections for a much better existence than hanging with us and our targets?" Ronald asks. The streets are pretty congested as people are bustling to and fro to get home from the tubes and buses. They move without much interference.

"Harold that is a good point. What is in for you besides the money?" Cash adds.

"To be honest with you. I like you two. I have no family and this could be my last great adventure. Even though I am blind I still have joy and the anticipation of what is to come. So I don't want to miss a thing."

So with that statement made they all shake hands and go their separate ways to again to meet up in America.

"I only have one request Pop?"

"What is that, Son?" He responds as the rain starts to fall even harder.

"Pop, can we go somewhere warm? Please. I am so bloody tired of being wet." Ronald says with a laugh.

"I have the perfect place in mind." He says and they both laugh as they head for the tube to make their way home to pack.

Chapter 16

Status

Ool and his crew mates sit in the common room waiting for the time to intersect with the time back on Zinghavi so they could see the random signals flow from the world. They have been away from the home world for three cycles in Earth terms roughly four months. The major goal was achieved and they had their help lined up to free their world. However, the stress of not being on their own planet is showing in each member. The charging chambers renew the minerals in their bodies and allows them to breathe easier as their planet. Gravity difference on this planet is strenuous on their bones and muscles since it is stronger. Laz and his attitude has even gone from flamboyant to sullen.

"Now before we can see the home world let's get something straight. Laz and Prill you two and I will have to stay longer. Slill will head back to make preparations for the

Pearl Agency on Zinghavi. Agreed?"

"No. It is better for me to stay. I need to pilot my ship

and I don't want to lose it due to subpar piloting." Slill says as

he polishes the intersecting wrench.

Laz and Prill knew this would happen since the

weaponry and armor has to be developed. It is not ideal, but

once they have the weapons they would head back and

further their development back home. Prill never looks up as

he has been in a maddening silence as his designs continue to

bewilder everyone. His feathers have a sheen due to the

perspiration being exuded in his concentration. The tips of

his feathers have changed in hue to red in his concentration.

"That's fine." Prill asks as his face peers over his

device looking at Ool, then back at his design.

"Ool what are we going to do after that. We can't talk to anyone back on Zinghavi, because we can't trust anyone to not trace our signal back here." Laz says.

"That is true, but we still can receive a signal. Lintoo always sends out a status call on the state of Zinghavi embedded in the President's speech. That is why we know that we are safe and no one is on our trail."

"Safe is one thing, but productive is better. We will really have to get the production on these designs started. It took so long to just get here and to understand how to work with Pearl Security. We need to get at least a prototype of these designs." Laz says as he finally picks his head up and waving the tablet with the protective suit on the screen.

There is a chime and the wall lights up with an aura of colors layering itself until the President of Zinghavi, Loo the Red. Standing there in his black tunic with cobalt stripes contrasting with his red feathers. As he preens for the camera the sound whines in and out as the signal is calibrated

by the buffer system. They miss the first part of the speech

due to it. As the sound returns,

"The civil unrest from Orenthia has been quelled to a

more manageable stage as of now. Thanks to the great

citizen Tul who has negotiated a limited truce for the next

four cycles. This season of peace awaits a new regime where

the change of our circumstance can allow our freedom.

Grossly underestimated potential of our citizens still not have

been tapped for our world to become free. There are still

souls that have left this world that will recalibrate our

existence, but patience gives us the ability to press on."

The rest of the speech covers the financial standings

of the provinces, power improvements and scientific

achievements. The panning of the camera shows the crowd

being stoic as they watched the speech from the conference

room. Tul is sitting on the front row with his pink tie with a satisfied look on his face. At the sight of his face, Ool shuts

off the screen. All of his compatriots look at him in shock.

"Why did you turn it off?" Slill asks.

"I heard what we needed to hear. We have four

cycles and they are waiting for us. Slill you have to map a

shorter route to save us at least one to two cycles. Bypass or

include more jumps to save the time. Did you see Tul?" Ool

says. He gets up and runs his fingers through his crown

feathers. Tul is embedded with the President's council to try

to find them. The time for him is running out and he hopes

Lintoo can stay hidden in plain sight.

Chapter 17

New Accommodations

Cash still marveled at the view of the Gulf of Mexico. He has seen the Atlantic Ocean as a boy till the last time he viewed it from the plane. The water in its dark blue hue was so imposing that he had no desire to touch let alone enter it. He and Ronald decided together to move not only to a warmer location, but a strategic one as well. In briefs with Ool and the crew that any team they would have to put together would have to be use to water and lots of it. The standard places like Florida or California were too big and the cost would not be beneficial to this new endeavor. So they decided to come to Texas, Corpus Christi to be exact. Small city with plenty of water access and an abundance of abandoned oil rigs to get their training on.

As he looks at the ocean from the office of their new home sipping his morning tea, he wishes that Arial could have seen it. The tear slips down from his eye and gets lost in his salt and pepper beard. The beard and its length are new as is the home they purchased on Ocean Drive a week ago. The transaction was handled prior to them coming and while they shuttered the house back in Shoreditch. Shamus said he would keep an eye on the place and all was covered for their departure. All that was brought were their beds and Arial's clothing. Just leaving it behind caused him to become ill and Ronald packed all the boxes so his father could relax. Their clothes were unnecessary here since the heavier clothing in this humid climate would be the death of them.

"Morning Pop. I have the files of possible team members from one of my old commanders from the UN Task Force." Ronald says as he comes into the office wearing workout clothes, black shorts and green Royal Marine t-shirt with the sleeves cutoff. Still slick with sweat from his five mile run up and down the drive. Prepping himself for action again has Ronald back to a laser focus of a task. He in turn

has ditched his goatee and just sports a mustache matching

his closer cropped hair.

Cash turns to his son while he wipes his face from the

sullen memories to more pressing business. His casual office

wear are linen slacks and light cotton shirt with customary

loafers, he is British after all.

"How many have they sent you, my boy?"

"Well, all out of the list we have twelve candidates.

Pretty solid candidates if I say so." He says and sits at the

small conference table in the office. The office sits in their

home along the back of the house. It is a four bedroom, five

bath house with a security wall. Luscious tropical plants and

palms decorate the landscape as they thrive in the Texas

heat. Office is appointed in woods and leathers with two flat

screen monitors linked to their computers.

"So what three are you looking at to fill out your first team?""

There had been heated discussions that finally persuaded Cash to "permit" Ronald to take the first team to Zinghavi. Their partnership had been defined after this decision. Ronald would handle all teams, training and logistics. Cash would handle the money and establishment of Earth born enterprises to further facilitate more stream of revenue and give returning teams jobs.

"Well, out of the twelve the three I have my eye on are all Americans."

"Why all Americans?"

"The reason is that I want to use Americans to avoid issues with visas and these three are really good."

"It's your call. So who are they?"

"The first one is waiting for us at the airport right now. So get your bag and we are headed to Colombia to meet our second candidate." Ronald says with a smile and jumps up to head out of the office.

"Wait what do you mean? We haven't even gotten settled in son. Now we are leaving to go to another country. Can't they come to us?"

"Yes, they could. But, the best way to judge a soldier is in his environment, not over a desk."

"Well, what do I need to bring?" Cash says as he is flustered and has given up on his breakfast tea.

"Bug spray. Plenty of bug spray and a hat."

Ronald packs his bag with jeans, long sleeved light Henley's and three pairs of boots. He jumps in the shower and allows himself to smile as the first step of many starts today. As he gets dressed in his new bedroom still surrounded by boxes, he looks out of his window into the front yard. The flowers are blooming and he sees the seagulls standing on the security wall. Shaking his hand and laughing that he was now living in Texas.

Cash cannot believe his son is dragging him to Colombia. The United States is only the second country he has been in and now Ronald is dragging him to his third in just two weeks. His main issue is not the travel, but his stomach still has not adjusted to the different food in Corpus Christi. The Mexican food and seafood has his stomach constantly queasy and close to water closet. So in Colombia he might as well not eat. While throwing in his slacks and shirts with one pair of boots and two pairs of loafers, he grabs his Tums and tea biscuits.

They both throw their bags in the back of their new silver Range Rover. Ronald slides behind the steering wheel, since Cash is not doing well with driving on the wrong side of the road. They follow Ocean Drive heading downtown and

merge to the left past the federal courthouse to IH 37. Jazz is

playing on the radio and they both are tense since the traffic

in Texas is more aggressive and congested. The first week

here they were honked at and given obscene gestures as they

were driving to slow. Merging on Highway 44 they reach the

private hanger entrance and park. Grabbing their bags, Cash

follows his son to the hangar office. He meets an employee

with Richard stitched on the front of a set of coveralls and

earmuffs around his neck. The office is basic with linoleum

floors and a counter. Jet fuel and exhaust has taken over the

office in a minute amount,

"Yes Sir, how can I help you?" Richard says with a

small lisp.

"Well yes you may. We have a flight scheduled with Lt

Commander Carla Jefferson. Is she ready?" Ronald asks as he

giggles watching Cash looking totally bewildered by the whole

143

seen. He looks so out of place with his pressed trousers, loose buttoned shirt and his straw fedora. The man named Ronald eyes open wide and he nods and excuses himself without a word.

"Son, why are you giggling?" He says as he peeks over the counter and starts walking around the office looking at pictures. On the wall he sees a young black woman in a green jumpsuit posing with jets, planes and helicopters. She is quite handsome.

"Do you think this lady flies all these aircraft?" Cash asks as apparently the question of the giggle was rhetorical.

"First, I am snickering not giggling. Young lasses giggle. To answer your question. We are heading to Colombia and you're dressed like we are going on holiday. Love the straw hat!" He says while both of them start laughing as Cash fix his brim comically. While they are both laughing, Richard comes back in.

"Flips is ready to see you. She is in the second hangar back." Richard says with a grin.

Ronald picks up his bag and laughs even harder while his father is standing their mouthing the word, Flips. He hands his father the file with the picture of the same lady on the wall on the front of it. Cash then looks to Richard who shrugs his shoulders and laughs. He shakes his head and walks back through the door he came through already. Cash is standing in the office wondering if he should grab the Tums out of his bag right now.

Chapter 18

Sweat

Ronald waits for his father to come out so they can walk together to meet their pilot. He puts his shades back in place as the Texas sun in May is merciless as a prelude to even a more oppressive summer. Their thicker British blood has not acclimated and both are drenched in sweat as they walk towards the hangar. Cash hands his bag to Ronald so he can speed read through the file before meeting their prospective teammate and employee. He pulls up short.

"Son, she is a bomber pilot or was a bomber pilot. However, on the pictures there were no bombers? What is the truth here?"

"Look at her personal biography. The woman can fly anything that leaves the ground; helicopters or planes. Grew up in Mission, Texas and her father was one of the only black farmers in the area. She taught herself how to fly a crop duster and from there she was known as a savant. A US Navy veteran who got the proverbial shaft from jets to just flying bombers. That is why she left."

They start walking again. The tarmac and the heat is baking from the sun and the asphalt. Walking past a number of smaller aircraft they are blinded by the glare from the windshields as the sun creeps from behind the only cloud.

"She is a fighter I see." Cash says as he holds up a photo of Carla posing with her third Golden Gloves title.

"Oh, yeah. She is dangerous in hand to hand and small arms. We will get her up to speed literally when it comes to ground principles."

"Why do we need a pilot, anyway?"

"I am not walking to the planet and let alone be constricted by Ool or any other pilot."

Cash rolls his eyes.

"She is going to fly a spaceship?"

"I bet she can. Do you want to put a quid on it?" Ronald says with a smile knowing his father's pension for playing the odds. Cash shakes his head and waves for them to get it in out of the heat.

They get to open hangar door and they both whistle in appreciation. In front of them is a magnificent piece of machinery. It is navy blue and white and every silver surface is polished. As they get a closer look the power of possibilities has given Ronald goosebumps.

"Gentleman, what are you doing is stalking and you can be arrested for that here in Texas." A slightly melodic voice calls out from interior of the plane. A woman climbs out from plane wearing a blue flight suit. She has medium brown skin, hair in braids with a radiant smile.

"Hello, gentleman my name is Carla Jefferson and I will be your pilot. My co-pilot Manual Ramirez is doing our pre-flight checks." She says and shakes each of their hands with a surprisingly firm grip that has Cash shaking his hand. As she grabs their bags they notice she is not that tall maybe five foot seven, but her frame is muscle under the t-shirt as she has the top of the flight suit tied at her waist.

They continue to walk around admiring the plane while simultaneously watching her. She is checking the flaps and linkages with a discerning eye. Moving with an elegant contained grace that belies a power that is intriguing.

"Excuse me Miss Jefferson what type of airplane is this?" Cash asks.

"Excuse me Mr. Cashmere, I did not realize you were British. What part?"

"We are from Shoreditch." Ronald says as he leans back into the conversation.

"Wow! This Texas heat must be brutal. Well to answer your question, she is a Piaggio P180/Avant EVO. She is propeller driven as you see mounted in the rear, upgraded of course. There are larger tanks instead of the standard that gives a longer flight distance up to 2000 miles. Plus an upgraded injection system to get our airspeed up to 400 knots. Reinforced landing gear for all terrain landings and all quadruple welds in structure."

"Quadruple welds? Isn't that excessive for such a beautiful plane?" Cash says and both Ronald and Carla look at him in bewilderment. She shakes he head and gives Ronald a look that prods him to tell his father the truth.

Ronald wipes off his brow and motions for Cash to follow him to the sitting area where an industrial fan is pushing cooler air from a portable chiller unit to a seating area. Cash sits and takes off his straw hat and fans himself. He knows there is something amiss and his nerves are tingling. Ronald has not told him the full story and he doesn't

understand why they can't fly commercial to Colombia versus

private plane.

"Pop. We are taking this private plane, because we

are flying to Colombia, but the jungles of Colombia. We are

using this plane, because our second candidate lives there

alone in seclusion. I talked to him by satellite phone and he is

willing to talk to us."

"Why do I have a feeling its worse than just being in a

jungle."

"Well...he lives in the middle of two warring cartels

and they have been known to shoot at planes. Even on some

occasions they have brought a few down." Ronald murmurs

the final statement and smiles. It is not possible for a man of

color to drain themselves pale, but the twinkle in his eyes

have truly dulled. Slowly Cash gets to his feet and makes a hurried strides towards Carla as she is zipping up her flight suit.

"Miss Carla."

"Call me Flips."

"Miss Carla. Can you fly us there and back? Why aren't we flying a jet? Do we have guns on the plane?" Cash rapid fires the questions at Carla and she responds with a smile. In turn she reaches out and grabs both of his hands in hers.

"Mr. Cashmere. I can fly us in and out of any place at any time. The reason I use Wanda is that she takes airplane fuel that is more readily available than jet fuel for where I fly. Lastly, what self-respecting Texan goes out without a gun or ten?" She says all this with a smile and hooks her arm into Cash's and walks him to the door and helps him in.

Ronald laughs to himself and heads in behind him. The inside of the plane is not luxurious with leather seats, but cloth seating for six people. There are two foot lockers on either side behind the seats. The cockpit is now occupied by Carla and her co-pilot Manual are making final checks. They are pulled from the hangar by Richard using a standard airline tug. Once in position the engines come to life with a throaty roar. The tremor and vibrations are synchronized as both engines fire in sync.

Ronald lays his head back in preparation for takeoff, however Cash is clearly agitated and is looking from the cockpit to his window.

"Pop, relax. We have a long flight."

Before Cash can respond he is slammed back into his seat as "Wanda" digs through the air on the runway as if "she" is fleeing gravity. The howl of the engines are in perfect harmony with Cash's scream of terror and

exhilaration!

Chapter 19

Poking Around

Tul sits in his cushion car awaiting the signal from Ash's lieutenant, Hurg the Merciless. He always wondered why the higher up Orethians had to have an embellishment with their name. Ash was Ash, but his tribe had the Merciless, Avenger or Obliterator stuck behind their single name. While still flicking his blade as it was his nervous habit, he wondered what befell Ool. He disappeared four cycles ago and no one knew where he was. His living quarters, job and associates turned up no information. His conspirator had bludgeoned and tortured anyone and everyone in the outer ring of circles that Ool was part of with no success.

As the car slowly rocked with the sway of the platform and wind whistling past the car he had to contemplate what to do next. Portraying himself as a loyal citizen and wanting the best for Zinghavi. The President was an untouchable entity, but someone in the senior staff knew the plans that Ool was laying.

"He was or never could be a fetching attraction for the females so that ruled out a third of the staff. Romantic entanglements and loss would and could be noticed." Tul murmured to himself. As he moved to flick his blade again, he stiffens at the movement outside his window, Hurg the Merciless. The Zinghavian towered over him at just under seven foot tall. Draped in the traditional scarves and kilt over worn boots made from eels, he stands there with unblinking black eyes. All Zinghavi look the same with exception to the females who were generally shorter in stature, but more vicious in their elimination of enemies. What made them more dangerous were their legs. They performed most of the hunting so this type of activity made them far quicker than their male counterparts. Hurg the Merciless paces in frustration, because he can't believe he has to meet with the heir of one of their previous masters.

"What do you want with me, Tul? You waste my time to talk of what?"

"Good to see you as well Hurg. I am doing well, so how are you?"

"Do not toy with me!" Hurg says as he whips around with his hand and slams his fist in the top of the cushion car. The massive dent is left in the metal while the car shimmies on its cushion from the violence. Tul glances at the dent while still standing his ground.

"You will pay for that indiscretion. The reason I called you was to get a message to Ash. No interplanetary calls to him directly on my part, so let him know that Ool has supporters in the inner chamber of the President. The missing number of the executives is becoming more apparent. No more interrogations by anyone."

157

"You no longer own us or tell us what to do. Are you asking us a question or is this a request?" Hurg says as he takes a step closer to Tul who still does not move.

"Consider it a request and I will get more information in a more subtle way."

"Fine. I will carry him this message." Hurg says and slinks back to the shadow of a building.

Tul watches him go. Behind his back his blade is open. There are things he will tolerate, but being threatened or abused by them is not one of them.

Chapter 20

Paradise

Ool and the crew gather in the ship's workshop after their recharging session this morning. The greatest call was made by the Cashmeres in coming to this Gulf of Mexico. Water was so warm and the salinity high enough that all of them have regained their color. The journey from England to the Gulf was not without issues. Due to the inability of using the atmosphere to cloak their movements, low altitude hop scotching from one island to the next. Finally settling in a group of abandoned oil rigs off the Texas coast.

"Ool we have completed a replica of the suit that Ronald requested. It has all the defensive measures, but it has made the suit to bulky for my liking." Laz says as he points to the oversized padding under the phez and cerrilic plates. The suit is reminiscent of a bobsledding, but the larger groups of the body has the padding supporting the plates.

"Laz, I have an idea. Why don't we lose the heavy padding and just do the plates with the neuro suit? It will eliminate the bulk and the neuro suit will allow them to understand where the damage and threat are." Prill says as he points out the suit he has been developing. His suit is the same color as Laz's suit and has a chain mail quality with the phez in ringlets.

"What is a neuro suit?" Ool asks.

"The neuro suit is designed as an underlayment of protection, however it has neuro receptors. These are the receptors." Prill says as he lifts the interior of the suit showing the pea size circles interconnected by barely tangible wires.

"It works as protection and signals through the humans nerves as pain. The initial assault will get their attention, however continued assaults will become more painful."

"What is the failure threshold? Also, what is the level of assault can it withstand?" Ool asks as he fingers the suit.

"My estimation would be at least ten shots in a focused area with our low velocity weapons. Levels I would say would be the long guns, but any shrapnel would not penetrate."

Laz stares at Prill with his conical eyes with a look of disrespect. He insisted they work apart and that decision has his intellect looking very mediocre.

"Laz, are you hearing me?" Prill asks again.

"What is it?" he says with disdain in his voice.

"Laz, your helmet is truly exceptional and I feel with these three combined is an exceptional tool for our..."

"Team. The word you are looking for is team. I like your thoughts. How does the helmet work?" Ool says.

"The helmet has its own oxygen supply. It scrubs the air and generates it by chlorophyll pods. The pods can give extended oxygen for up to five days. There is a display that calculates elevation, speed and targeting. All helmets will have communication links at lower frequencies that are not used on Zinghavi. It stays shaded so no one can be seen." Laz says with a smile as his work is appreciated. As he stands admiring the helmet, he does not see the nudge Ool gives Prill. He understands that Prill knows his work associate well.

"Have any of the weapons been prepared?"

"Yes. We have the assault weapons modified for propellant discharges. Velocities are slower and the rifling in the barrels widened to allow a smooth release, potentially."

"Potentially?"

"Ool, do you really expect us to fire a weapon on our ship under water?" Prill says with a laugh. Then with his laughter the others join in.

"I guess not." Ool says with a shake of his head.

Slill enters the workshop mid laughter. He scans the room and shakes his head. All laughter starts to taper off as Slill does not smile and waits for the uncomfortable silence to kick in.

"Pod we have an issue. These two have used up our stores of phez, so we have an issue with designing ammunition." Slill says and walks in to take a seat. The mood in the room has shifted and all take a seat.

"Well here on Earth what do they use for projectiles in their weaponry?" Ool asks.

"They use metal, it is called "lead". Laz says in a confident tone as if the problem is solved.

"That is correct, but the hides on the Orethians is impervious to lower based metals. This coupled with the slower velocity propellant fueled weapons will not cause any damage. So we have to come up with something lighter and not a metal." Slill says with a drone.

"He is correct. This is certainly an issue." Prill says.

"This is a problem we will need help to solve." Ool says and gets up as the others ponder what the next step will be.

Chapter 21

Wanda

The P180 has finally leveled off cruising altitude and the screaming stopped about five minutes after takeoff. However, the laughter has dribbled off into giggles as Ronald watches his Pop. Cash is covered in sweat and has a slight tremor in his forearms as his hands grip the armrests. His Pop smiles as the adrenaline tapers off.

"Pop, you okay? I never knew you had that type of range." Ronald says

"If I keep flying with this young lady in this fashion, I will be an operatic soprano." He says as he laughs at his own behavior.

The plane banks to the right as the head towards their destination for their first leg of the flight. Engines drop in an octave as they are set to cruising speed. Sunlight continues to pour through the cabin and the atmosphere is quiet. The cockpit door opens and Carla walks out. She has wide grin on her face as the laughter comes to her and Ronald as Cash sheepishly grins.

"Mr. Cashmere, I thought my windshield was going to crack when you hit that F sharp!"

"The window may have not cracked, but sides ache from all the hysterics my Pop was putting on."

Carla steps to a door and opens it. Cool air comes into the cabin.

"Can I get you gentleman something to drink? I have sandwiches for later."

"I would like a bottle of water, please." Cash says. Ronald nods his head for the same and soon they both have Core water bottle in hand.

Carla takes a seat and both men turn around so they are all face to face.

"So Ronald. You got in touch with me through Commander Runnels. He says you have a job besides this one?"

"You are absolutely correct. However, I have a question before I answer yours. How is it possible for a military veteran to own a plane this nice?"

"Excuse, my son and his forwardness."

"Oh, never you mind that forwardness. I am glad to answer that question. Ronald, I have flown everything from helicopters, planes and even my favorite single engine crop dusters. When you have those skills, people will pay you for a trip or a mission. I don't run drugs and you know I don't fly terrorists. This plane was paid for by a certain company in for retrieving its CEO and family from a country under siege."

"Would that country have sand or snow?" Ronald asks. As he leans back he knows we exactly what the scenario was.

"Snow."

Cash looks from one to the other waiting.

"That was quite a brave endeavor. How were the going away fireworks?"

"Sheila my baby before Wanda here gave up the ghost on that party. Limped all the way back to a more friendly country. This was a gift in her remembrance."

"So this beauty is named Wanda?" Cash asks.

"Why Wanda? If I may ask."

"There was this lady I saw in Alabama named Wanda. She stood on this street corner everyday proclaiming that Jesus loved you. This was not the best spot in town, but her love for the people touched me. You know in the end to be loved no matter who you are or what you are? This lady will never measure up to that lady." Carla says as she reclines back in her seat.

The heaviness of that moment requires a little bit of silence. After a couple of beats, Ronald starts the pitch.

"Carla, we have a benefactor that needs us to do a job. That job is in that sort of gray area. I am being up front. It is helping an entity to escape from oppression. There will be travel and it will be extensive." Ronald says as he leans forward in his seat.

"Gray has many shades. Is it a light gray or a smoke gray that is almost black?" Carla asks with an edge of curiosity.

"I would say a medium gray." Cash says as he sips his water. He is letting Ronald take the lead with his fellow veterans. Cash did not serve due to his own obligations with his father.

"This type of gray work pays well?"

"Yes it does and I would like to extend a preliminary invitation. After this trip I would like for you to visit our benefactors to get the full story."

"You have my attention and I am curious as well."

After the acceptance of their invitation "potentially" she heads back to the cockpit to relieve Manual. He heads back and gives the Cashmeres a nod as he hits the head. At a glance Mr. Ramirez isn't just some co-pilot, as Cash spots shrapnel scars on the right side of his face. He tries to hide them by letting his hair grow out. As he ducks down to get into the bathroom he is at least half a head shorter than Ronald, but shoulders as wide as a wardrobe. After the water turns off, he heads back out. Cash makes the move before Ronald can stop him.

"Excuse me, Mr. Ramirez."

"Yes Sir." The large man says as he stops in his tracks without turning around.

"Could we speak to you for a minute?"

Ronald has removed the earphones that he had just put on perplexed by what is going on. He sits up in his seat and scratches his beard trying to understand what is going on. Pop is sitting on the edge of his seat trying to get the co-pilot's attention.

"What's going on Pop?" He says as he sees the massive man for the first time. The man is shorter than he is, but the frame is so muscular that his flight suit is rolled at the legs. The suit is for a much taller man but his frame couldn't stand it.

"Gentleman. I have to get back to the cockpit. Can we speak later because we have a refueling stop scheduled in two hours?" He says and continues to the cockpit with a Hispanic lilt to his words.

171

Chapter 22

Surprise

Harold hears the phone ringing to his left. On instinct he fingers the braille face on his watch. It is 1 am and he knows who is exactly calling. He does nothing, but snap his fingers. Cassius his faithful guide dog brings the phone to him on its special tether so he can answer the phone. His was the third in an encrypted set and no taps or data could not break the encryption without fingerprints from all three men.

"Yes, Mr. Ool." Harold says as he answers the phone. He strokes Cassius for bringing him the phone and hand signals for him to bring him his water bottle. He can hear the gentle crush of the water bottle between Cassius' powerful jaws. The bottle is in his hand and Harold reclines back in his chair for the conversation.

"Good evening, Mr. Harold. How is the weather back in England?"

"Cold and that is all I can tell you, Sir. What do you need me to do?"

"Not a task, but information. We have tried repeatedly to reach the Cashmeres and have not had any success."

Harold strokes the scars around his eyes from the failed surgeries to keep away the darkness. All those surgeries and all he has left is the scars and the darkness.

"Remember they are gathering their team, so they are travelling. Maybe I can help?" He says and sits up to a sitting position then to his feet.

"Well, Harold this is about ammunition."

"New ammunition or Earth ammunition?" He says as he gets to the kitchen counting his steps. Hunger at 1 am would cause him to get in the gym for more than he was willing to pay. But, all he had was time anyway.

"This is about the new ammunition. The weight of the Earth ammunition is not able to be propelled by the modified weapons. We need something lighter, but the lighter metals will not inflict damage. Increasing the propellant charges overheats the weapons and jams. Is there something we are missing?"

Harold probes his mind and rocks on his bare feet on the ceramic tiles. His mind kicks this question back and forth.

"Have you tried aluminum?"

"Yes and the projectiles flatten."

"How about titanium?"

"Too heavy."

"I thought you were using the phez?"

"Our limited supply is being used in the protection of the team. There is no surplus to make an infinite amount of ammunition."

Harold moves to get to the refrigerator and opens it to grab a shake. As he turns the slickness of the tile betrays him and his great toe is sliced. The pain is not apparent, but the heat of his blood mingling with the slickness of the tile. He grunts.

"How about ceramic? So before you ask ceramic is made from clay. It has a hardness of stainless steel without the weight." Harold says as he limps towards his bathroom to take care of his bleeding toe. He feels the trail of blood he is leaving dripping into the grains of his hardwood floors. There are thirteen steps to the bathroom from the kitchen and he turns right at step thirteen. The tub is straight ahead and the sink with the cabinet is to his left. The alcohol and the gauze are in the bottom of the sink on the right hand side. He reaches down and grabs both of them. Sitting on the side of the tub he listens to Prill drone on about the negative assessment of ceramic.

"I understand what is wrong with using it, but what about it is plentiful. Think about how to make it work or better yet, ask the Cashmeres the same question."

"Do not be upset with us my friend. We are just trying to solve a problem. Any idea when they will be back?"

"No. However, I would keep trying to contact them since time is about to become an issue."

"That is true and indeed we will continue to try. Take care of your injury my friend. We will be in touch." Ool says and hangs up the line.

Cassius is whimpering at the bathroom door as he smells the blood.

"Don't worry old boy. It is just a cut nothing to worry about." Harold says as he gets the bleeding to stop and winces from the alcohol.

Chapter 23

Machetes and Mosquitos

After making a short fueling stop in Mexico City the crew continues southeasterly trek to Colombia. Ronald and Cash sleep peacefully as the plane drones on. They all got a good stretch in Mexico City and lunch of roasted corn and grilled steak bought from airport vendors. Rest was at a premium before the touched down in Colombia. While the Cashmeres slept another conversation was being had in the cockpit.

"So they have a job for me and it seems pretty big. Looking at their file we are going to Colombia to recruit another soldier named Matta. Seems pretty big. You want in on it?" Carla says as she trims the flaps after climbing an extra 2000 feet.

"Not sure. The older one."

"Cash. The older one is named Ronald Cashmere III and that is his son Ronald Cashmere IV. Both Brits and the son Ronald was British Special Forces. He was part of the UN Forces in Africa and I checked my channels and he is legit. They have some operation they are interested in me for. I heard them talking to you? They offer you?"

Manual checks the flight path and the wind speed before answering. Since him being such a powerful man with many capabilities he is very thoughtful before he says anything. Carla is use to this idiosyncrasy, so she waits as he gathers his thoughts.

"Yea, they got my attention and I put them off till later."

"If I push for you and the deal includes you?"

"Nope. I have too many things going on with my family, so I will not go on no extended Op."

"Well, I know you so I am not going to push. But, if it's good…"

"Don't tell me and I got your back if you take it. Plus, me and Wanda can get our groove on." Manual says with a wink and rubs his hand across the dashboard."

Carla rolls her eyes and waggles the plane to the left. That in turn gets a startled scream from Cash. The next three hours are uneventful as they get closer to their final destination. The sun is rising on the eastern horizon and the rolling greens over the mountains of the border of Colombia are still dark beneath them.

"Ronald could you come up here, please." Carla says over the plane's intercom. There is a rumble and a pop then he appears.

"What was that pop?"

"Craggy knees from a lot of futbol and walking everywhere with her Majesty's service." He responds with a laugh. All three laugh as they all have the same aches and pains.

"Seriously I am looking these coordinates and are we going to Bogota?"

Manual groans.

"Manual, old chap. We are not going to Bogota. Take the heading southwesterly course for 482 kilometers. There will be a clearing and they will pop smoke for the airstrip."

"Understand. Setting course to 4.6097 degrees S by 74.0817 degrees W past Bogota 482 kilometers." Manual repeats the instructions.

"That is correct."

The plane banks and corrects to the right course heading under the steady hands of Carla. The cockpit is refined in the finishes of a luxury car. Not wood finishes, but the black and chrome type of finishes. As Ronald continues to stoop his large frame in the doorway he looks out of the window at the jungle below.

"Who is them? Also, is it cool landing or warm?" Carla asks as she glances at Ronald over her right shoulder.

Ronald strokes his beard and answers rather quickly.

"Definitely warm. Do you have any party favors for that occasion?"

Manual cracks the first smile he has seen. They are perfectly white and straight. Also, for the first time he sees his whole face. Manual is in his early thirties and the shrapnel is not only on his face, but also his neck. Letting his black hair grow thick to cover his scarred cauliflower ear.

"I have just the thing I have been wanting to try. Permission to go back?" Manual says with the exuberance of a kid at Christmas. Carla rolls her eyes and he is gone.

Pushing past Ronald he heads to the locker behind the seats.

They both laugh. Ronald looks and sees the lid open up and

he gasps in surprise. Before him there is a 50 caliber machine

gun with tripod laying in there. Once he removes that he has

Cash's full attention.

He places the gun on the opposite locker and gets the

gun oil out to prep the weapon. As he slides the action, his

eyes twinkle with excitement.

"Excuse me Ronald. Why is Mr. Ramirez pulling out

that instrument of death?" Cash asks as he gets on his feet as

they watch the man work.

"I thought we were going to Colombia? How are we

getting that through customs?"

"Pop, we are headed to Colombia, but the jungles of

Colombia." Ronald says with a shrug.

"Son, you could have left me at home. I am not a jungle strolling person. I don't even have shoes or clothes for that!" Cash says as sweat comes out as a sheen on his bald head in the cold plane. Ronald places both hand on his father's shoulders.

"Pop, you are staying with the plane. The reason I didn't leave you, because we are partners. I need you to back up Mr. Ramirez and I will be the one slogging through the jungle."

A voice calls out behind him.

"Mr. Cashmere I will keep an eye on him. Also, by the way I hate the jungle!"

"Since we all have our assignments. Ronald would you mind helping me move my little pea shooter back so I can get your jungle gear ready. After getting Cash to settle down, Ronald helps move the 50 Cal back. Opening the next locker there lies a treasure trove of knives, machetes, AR-15 machine guns, Glocks and cans of ammunition. There is low whistle and giggling from Manual. This man has turned from sullen to jovial in the last two hours.

"How far are we out?" Ronald asks.

"Sixty minutes." Carla says from the cockpit. At that Ronald goes in his pack and pulls out his satellite phone. He punches in a code and receives a response.

"Carla, look for smoke. Green is clear and orange is warm."

"Warm? We are heading to the jungle of course it is warm." Cash says while his nervousness continues to percolate.

"Okay. Carla can you hear me?" She responds with a thumbs up.

"Now we are going to have a meeting with Rodrigo Matta. He is Colombian by race, but an American by birth.

He was born in Florida. After serving one tour in the Army,

he became DEA for the next eight years. He moved here to

jungle, because his family's farm is where he wanted to be.

There are two cartels that try to push them off this land and

his mission is to keep this strip free. We will land at the strip

three miles out from the farm. We will walk in for this

meeting. Pop and Manual will keep trespassers off of

Wanda's back." Ronald says and ends with a smile.

Weapons are checked at least three times. Packs are

checked and filled with medical kits. Water is distributed and

lightweight bulletproof vests are checked and fitted. Manual

relieves Carla in the cockpit and she changes into more

friendly jungle gear; cargo pants, long sleeve lightweight shirt

and snake boots.

"Pop follow Manual's lead. You play second line of

defense. Pick off any strays that don't get obliterated with his new toy. If it gets to heavy use the satellite phone and we will be here."

"You get in and get out. By the way I get to pick the next assignment. I don't like being pickled!"

Ronald grips his father's hand as he settles back into his seat.

"Gentlemen, we have red smoke!" Carla says from the cockpit.

As they start their descent, Cash's cellphone chimes with a message. He picks it from his shirt pocket as the plane starts its turn to line up with the grassy runway. He holds the phone away so he can see it since his reading glasses are in his bag. He refuses to unbuckle with Carla at the controls. As he tries to focus the descent is accelerating.

"Ronald what do you know about ceramics?"

"Ceramics? You mean like the cats Mum had?"

"I guess. Here look at this? Carla, why are we going faster going down just like going up?" Cash grunts as his stomach is misplaced.

"Appears to be some issues with ammunition. Wondering about ceramic bullets? Something I will run by our new friend Mr. Ramirez. Then suddenly they all become weightless.

Chapter 24

Vanished

Every week on alternating days Dolores and Randall make the leisurely drive to the East End to check on the status of the Cashmere garage. At first it was a curiosity to see if the men would reappear after the altercation with Gus and his departed henchman. They have seen all of the police tape and long weeks of investigators poking around. This transitioned to construction crews removing the debris and new construction starting. Now for the last five months the Cashmeres have not been seen anywhere in the city.

"Randall, please take me through Shoreditch." Dolores calls from the back of the Range Rover. She is dressed impeccably as ever. Her raven hair tied into a top knot while wearing a Gucci pants suit with matching heels. She is leaned against the back passenger door gazing at the construction looking for any sign of the men. This hunt is not for revenge, but has turned into an obsession.

"Ma'am, we have had men sitting on their home for five months. There has been no movement except with an occasional visit from their cousin, a family attorney." Randall says from the seat in front of her.

"Randall, tell me the truth. Did you have them killed despite my orders?" She says with a hint of malice.

"No. I would never do that and this is the same question you ask every week. This is same answer I give every week. They are in the wind due to the two circumstances that they were victim too."

They ride in silence as the truck rolls towards Shoreditch. The music wafts throughout the vehicle and Adele's voice soothes the average person's ear. However, on this occasion it awakens an idea for Dolores.

"Do you have a number for them?"

"Well, yes. There has been no activity on those lines in the same amount of time."

"What about the attorney's phone? He has been checking with them. He has too."

There is a silence from the front seat. Apparently no one thought about making that connection. Randall takes his phone from his pocket and keys a button. There is a short conversation and he hangs up.

"By the time we get there we will have one."

They ride and pass through the areas of London that slightly depresses until they reach Shoreditch. As they pass the home of the Cashmeres, Randall phone rings. The words are few and he hangs up. He passes the phone back to Dolores. She keys the number on the touch screen and waits. The phone rings and then it is answered. As she listens she snatches the phone from her ear. What has her surprised is

the sound of an airplane and a husky voice screaming.

Randall hits the breaks suddenly and looks in the rearview

mirror. Their eyes meet and neither know what to say.

Chapter 25

Stubborn

Carla lands the plane smoothly after stalling at the last 800 feet and pulling up. Landing the plane like a flop shot on a golf course and rolling down the runway. Positioning the plane where the nose is facing away from the mountain and using a rock formation to the left as a shield. All personnel storm out of the plane and set up the 50 caliber with tripod. Carla unlatches bulletproof shields from the aft section. Ronald helps stake them in and they both return to the plane to grab their gear. There is a motor whine in the distance.

"Look here is the radio, Manual. We are on channel 4." Carla says as she tucks her radio to the strap on her backpack. She surveys the surroundings and sees nothing, but jungle. The air is so thick that all of them are soaked in sweat within this first ten minutes. Ronald check his compass and gets his bearing as well.

"We are heading south approximately three miles. We have company coming from the north so keep alert. Manual keep an eye on my Pop. He gets kind of cavalier in a gunfight." Ronald says with a wink.

"Carla, you watch out for Ronald there. He is way too happy. I got your Dad."

Ronald and Carla start to head out, but Ronald stops and turns back.

"Manual, how would you make a ceramic bullet?"

Both Carla and Manual look at him confused. Ronald then turns and starts to jog at a steady clip with Carla at his heels. Cash and Manual cinch up their vests and check their weapons. The whining is getting louder and it is joined by the sound of heavy trucks as well. They get low and hunker down behind the panels.

"What is this about ceramic bullets?" Manual says without looking at Cash. Cash being the taller man is behind him and to the left. The anticipation of the fight has both of them feeling really calm.

"It is the operation we were talking about with Carla."

"Why don't you say Flips?"

"We're British and she is a lady."

"A lady, okay."

Mosquitos buzz around their ears and the sun is still rising. The mist from the dew is still hanging low over the landing strip. There is no sound as the jungle waits for the battle as well.

"Manual I may have a job for you?"

"I am not traveling for a long time. My family needs me. Heads up one o'clock."

Cash turns and sees what Manual sees. Off in the distance he sees a young man peer through the canopy. He waves and is joined by four other men. They start to fan out and head towards them. In their position with the panels they are temporarily invisible.

"So are we going to shoot?" Cash whispers through the mist to Manual. The group of men are coming in and out of focus through the mist. Never looking away from his field of vision, Manual shakes his head. Both of his hands rest in his lap and not on the weapon. The men stop coming forward and branch back off into the jungle.

"They are going to set an ambush for whoever comes back. That's when we will shoot. Manual clicks the radio two times in long bursts. This was the designated signal for company at the air field.

Ronald has slowed after crossing the small stream and hears the second burst. Carla answers with one long burst as

195

she comes back to him. He may be the taller of the two, but the pilot moves with the skill of a jackrabbit. Instead of striding through the jungle, she hops and launches off of rocks and logs.

"How in the world do you keep that scatter shot pace up? That would completely tucker me out and unbelievably sore?" Ronald asks as he gasps for air. The air is thick with humidity and the altitude. He takes a gulp from his water bottle.

"Hunting rabbits in Boutte Louisiana. During my first couple of years out I traveled and that was one of my stops. Rabbits in the swamp don't like getting shot, so chasing them down you have to move. Plus, I hate having wet socks." She says with a laugh. Checking her compass and her distance tracker on her watch.

"We are about half a mile away."

They had been following a foot path then an upward

trail towards the farm. The vegetation had been thinned and

passed a few old fence posts. Before they continue they

survey their surroundings.

"That guy can move."

"What do you mean?" Ronald says.

"He popped smoke and was able to make it all the

way back to his farm. We are humping the last sixteen

minutes and still have to go up hill."

"You're right! That's too far to run!" A voice says from

above. Both guns swing as one up to the voice. In the tree's

foliage they see the khaki pants dangling from the branch. In

the pants is a lean powerfully man sporting long hair and an

even longer beard black in color. He is wearing a white tee

shirt and a tactical vest. As they continue to have their guns

aimed, he slides down the trunk with the nimbleness of a

gymnast. He smiles at them both as the guns still don't move.

"Ronald, I invite you to my home and you still want to shoot me?" The man says as he takes off his hat and bows deeply to both of them. He is carrying his on assault rifle, pistol and machete. He is taller than Ronald, but his flexibility is uncanny. His long hair with his bow is touching the stream. Suddenly with a flick his head shoots up with his hair and water is flung into their eyes. Then as their eyes clear he is gone. As they attempt to track him, they hear him behind them. His arms are across his chest and his weapons are still put away.

"Now if I wanted to kill you I could have. Now, my name is Rodrigo Matta, but you can call me Rod." He says with an outstretched hand. Ronald takes the hand and shakes it while slinging his weapon over his shoulder. The grip is solid and the hand is heavily calloused. Carla shakes his hand as well and starts to look around as they are in the open.

"Don't worry about the cartel. I have killed enough of them and they know the boundaries of my land. So we are good for a few minutes. What do you need me for?"

As they get off of the path and talk under the shade of the trees. Ronald tells him the same introduction to a possible operation, just as he had with Carla. However, instead of being distracted with the task of flying a plane, Rod has better questions.

"Okay Ronald. You want me for an operation in some gray work? Freeing the people and being hailed as heroes is not me. You want me to give up all of this for what?" Rod says.

Carla listens as well for her own enlightenment. Ronald pauses thinking how much he should say, but he does not want to cheat them either.

"Okay, as a teaser or incentive. It pays up to 3.5 million dollars per year on a two year contract that will pay a maximum of 7 million dollars. Signing on is two years, period."

The only sound between them is the running water and the buzz of mosquitoes. Carla and Rod look at each other, then shift their gazes to Ronald with more questions. But, the possibility of that type of payday has kept them quiet. Their meeting is broken up with three quick bursts and the sound of heavy machine gunfire from over the hill.

Chapter 26

Lead Poisoning

Racing back to the airfield with Rod in the lead moving like a wide receiver with Carla zig zagging behind him. Ronald is bringing up and covering the rear as they head back to the air field. The thump of the 50 Cal has birds and small animals scurrying for cover. As they get to the top of the hill, Rod stops and curses. Down below them there are soldiers trying to flank the plane. Unbelievably they are being pushed back by the unforgiving gun and each flanking unit mowed down by an assault rifle.

Since coming up behind the baffled soldiers and their focus on the prize of the airplane, their rear is exposed.

"Look, Manual we are here. We are at the top of the hill and will come in from the east. Keep your fire south and west. We will clean up the east." Ronald says in the radio.

"Got it! We had this under control!" Cash says as they all see at least three men sawed in half on a strafing run.

"Who is that? He sounds happy?" Rod asks.

"That's me Pop. Let's get down there before he hurts himself." Ronald says with no humor and leads the way while being flanked by Carla and Rod. As they get moving there is movement in front of them and they start picking off the stragglers and cowards. There is no need to be quiet since the big gun is deafening everyone. Big guns are intimidating not just by the destruction, but the sound instills fear. Brass is glittering as sunlight hits it as it arcs from the chamber after delivering its message. Bodies are falling and diving for cover at each arc of the gun. There is smatterings of screams and Spanish in the air surrounding the airfield.

Simultaneously, unbeknownst to those pressing trying to get to the airplane, compadres are falling equally as fast on the east. Carla and Rod continue to press through the jungle and gain more ground. As Ronald steps over the downed

men they are dressed in rags, but have high end weaponry.

Assault rifles and pistols lay scattered everywhere. Up ahead

around near the rock formation blocking the side of the

plane, there is a straggler moving into position with a rocket

propelled grenade launcher. He is at the blind side of Manual

and Cash and a shot from there will destroy the plane and

them. Ronald sees him and in one motion he takes the shot.

One hundred yards out without a scope, the bullet passes

between Carla and Manual into the man's skull. The delay of

the sound comes behind the blossom of brain matter. Man

and RPG clatter harmlessly down the rocks.

"Don't you ever do that again!" Carla hisses. Then

presses on to close the distance. Fighters realizing there is

nothing to gain now as they are pressed back. Ronald calls on

the radio notifying the others they are coming across their

blind side. They slide down the rocks and come from the rear under the tail. When they catch sight of the two, they all laugh.

Cash is smiling from ear to ear with cuts to the top of his ear and a swollen eye. His fine clothes are soaked with blood from small nicks and cuts from rock shrapnel. Manual does not look back and just gives a thumbs up. He is bleeding from his shoulder from a graze as the blood is just trickling.

"Okay, you two! Since you have had your fun, let's get a move on. We have awakened every gun in the next three valleys. I will start pre-flight checks." Carla says then turns and punches Ronald in the gut. He grunts and tries to catch his breath. Cash hops up in surprise and empty shells fall from his clothes.

"What was that for?" Cash asks as Carla presses past him and enters the plane.

"It was a good shot." Rod says and Cash turns in surprise not realizing they had a new member. Manual turns his head slightly at the new voice as well. Ronald has caught his wind and stands up straight.

"Pop, I had bad manners and took a shot with her and Rod here in my line of sight without a warning. It is deserved. Rod this is my Pop, Ronald Cashmere III and Manual Ramirez. This gentlemen is Rodrigo Matta, the reason you two got to bond over fireworks."

Hands and nods are passed between the men.

"Manual, you and Pop wrap up the big gun and all the other weapons. I will stand guard and Rod if you wouldn't mind take the rock side?"

"Not a problem. They will regroup, but the heaviness of the losses will make them hesitate. Can't believe I am losing my farm." Rod says and turns to climb the rocks.

As the gear is being put up and flight check is being done, Ronald heads out with Rod to make sure they are clear.

The runway has bodies strewn about and they take turns

pulling them from the path. As they work they hear the

generator start to heat up the engines.

"Rod, how many acres do you own here?"

"Well, I own 200 acres. Are you serious about that

type of money? I do not run drugs and I am not a thief." He

says as they head back towards the plane.

"So if you come what about your animals?"

"Animals! They are no more animals left, just one

chicken." He says in a serious tone. Ronald pauses and

before he can say anything there is a rumble of motors in the

distance. Without another word they run back to the plane

as the engines start. They all grab a seat and Wanda begins

to roll.

"Everyone hold one! We are leaving hot!" Carla yells

over her shoulder. She removes her foot from the brake is

accelerating down the runaway. She is at full speed and the

engines are growling like two caged bears. The three men in

the cabin are slammed back in their seats. Cash is not

screaming, but the death grip on the seats expresses his

feelings.

Hurtling down the runway the bumping drops away

suddenly as do their stomachs. The mountains are coming up

fast and there is no way she is going to clear them. Ronald

peeks through the cockpit to see it coming. She knows they

would not make it and tips Wanda on a wing and slices

through the valley. As the plane slaloms through the valley

altitude is steadily being gained. Flashes of light come from

the canopy as fighters take parting shots. Once the right

altitude is achieved and they are at a cruising speed, when

Cash takes a breath.

"It was easier being shot at. Carla I love you, but this

is my last flight with you." Cash says with a laugh. The jittery laughter is a result of adrenaline levels bottoming out after all the fighting and flying.

"I love you too, Baby." Carla says with a giggle and she comes back into the cabin. Now let me take a look at you." She says and grabs the med kit from the pack. As she patches the nicks and cuts with alcohol and antibiotic ointment. Ronald and Rod do the same to each other. Any soldier has to patch a buddy up and it is done in return.

"Now about the animals on your farm. I think I misheard you, how many did you leave?' Ronald asks.

"You heard right. I only had one chicken left."

All passengers stopped and gape at Rod. Manual turns his head.

"Did he say one chicken?"

"Yes. Now to tell the truth if you hadn't come, it was dinner." This is said with a smile and a wink.

"We risked our lives for you being stubborn over a chicken?" Carla says with amazement in her voice.

"No one ever asked me what I had. You guys asked for a meeting. So if you wanted to meet with me, come to me." Rod says with indignity in his voice.

"So are you willing to have a more civilized meeting about this operation? If not I am more than sure Carla has no problem dropping you off before we get to the US?" Ronald says as he has placed the last bandage on his own hand. Carla nods her head as she is leaning against the bulkhead.

"Sure. But, can we stop somewhere I can get a haircut and clean clothes." Rod answers.

Chapter 27

Late Night

After landing in Corpus Christi the crew splits up. The damage to the plane is superficial and Carla stays back with a repair crew to make the repairs. Cash pays Carla the agreed upon fees plus a thirty percent tip for all the aggravation. He then gives Rod an envelope to handle his personal affairs. Manual excuses himself in preparation for the next pick up.

"Ronald, you asked me a question while in Colombia." Manual says as he finally looks at Ronald in his eyes. His comfort level has risen especially over the last five days.

"Yes, I did. What do you think?" Ronald says as he is amazed that the question remained in his head in spite of the turmoil.

"It is possible. But, what caliber of bullet, distance you are trying to achieve and most important what is it for?"

"If you can solve that problem, you will be amazed for what is for, my friend." Ronald tells Manual and turns to leave.

"Mr. Ramirez, thank you for keeping me safe. Also, what I have to offer is a job as well. However, it will be with me here in Texas with some travel. Ronald still needs that help, but I need you with me. Think about it." Cash says and gives Manual a hearty handshake. He turns and slaps his son on the back and heads to the truck.

The Cashmeres get to their truck and get in. Once they sit in their seats the pain and soreness of the past five days has set in. Ronald starts the truck and turns the air conditioning on full blast.

"Well son, how was your trip?" Cash says with a laugh as he rubs his hand over his bandaged and stubble on his head.

"Well Pop. I think I have two solid soldiers. My question is what do you see in Manual Ramirez?"

"He is workhorse, plain and simple. That workhorse is a genius under fire and in a conversation. The question of the ceramic bullet stayed his head and he has a solution. Son, you are going to be leaving me and I need strong men around me."

The heaviness of the potential separation has silenced both men. Ronald gets the truck in gear and heads back to their house. Since they came in the late evening the temperature is not as brutal. Traffic is moderate as they get off of IH-37 and make their way to Ocean Drive. Both of them being hungry they make a call for takeout from the Oyster Bar. Picking up their order on Water Street, they finally head home. Then a phone beeps from the backseat.

"Whose telephone is that?" Cash says as he looks at his phone and Ronald's next to the gear shift. The phone beeps again and Cash reaches his bag first. Rummaging

through his pack there is no phone, then it beeps again.

Ronald's bag is the one beeping.

"Son it's your bag." Cash grabs the bag and fishes

through it until he finds the phone. He gets the phone out

and realizes it is the old phone from England. Looking at the

screen he sees there is a message.

"Ronald, why is your old phone in your bag?"

Ronald grips the steering wheel and lets out a slow

breath. He then strokes his beard and continues to drive. His

eyes start to get a little misty then he clears his throat.

"The reason I have the phone is that I could not

transfer the pictures of me Mum to my new phone. So I carry

it so I can see it at least once a day. I know I should have left

it, but I didn't."

Cash is speechless and grabs the locket around his neck. His picture and hers were over his heart so he knew the feeling. All he can do is squeeze his son's shoulder as he drives. Then he realizes there is a message.

"Ronald, there is a message. I am going to play it?"

There is silence then a woman's voice starts to speak with a distinct British accent and something else.

"Ronald this is Dolores Thakur. You may not remember me, but we went to preparatory school together. You may not remember me, although you did dance with me at the formal in our tenth year. If you could give me a call back or text. Be well." The voice says then ends.

"Pop, I remember her, but why is she calling me now? It has been eighteen years since then."

Cash pulls out his reading glasses to better see the time stamp. As he is able to see it now, he realizes that the

214

call came in while they were in Colombia. No need in bringing that up and an old flame trying to hook his son is no matter.

"You know what son. It took her twenty years to track you down, so she can wait a little longer. Let's get home. I loathe eating soggy fish." Cash says as he shakes the take out container.

Ronald turns into the driveway and puts in the code to get in. They pull into the garage and head into the house. Lights are turned on and they sit their bags down in the kitchen. Cash pulls out plates and silverware to sit down and eat.

"I am so tired of eating out of foam and plastic." Cash says as he sets the table. Ronald goes into the wine chiller and grabs a bottle Pinot Grigio with two glasses. The plates are set and food split up between the both of them. They both eat and silence is deafening so Ronald grabs the remote and turn on some music. Jazz wafts around them and the

mood lightens. Once they have finished eating and the dishes

in the dishwasher, they both head to their own spaces.

Exhausted Ronald hits the shower and scrubs the last

five days off his skin and under his nails. Standing in the

mirror he looks himself over before he shaves. There are

bruises and scrapes he has to tend to before he heads to bed.

He smiles to himself as the past days run through his mind.

He can't believe this is happening.

"We have millions in the bank and getting paid to do

this?" He says to himself.

After shaving and more first aid, he heads to bed. The

bedroom is an upgrade from the old home in London. As he

stretches out on the king size bed and starts to drift off, his

last thought is of Dolores in a cream colored formal.

Shave, shower and first aid, Cash is on his side of the

bed. His wife still has her side and her same closet. His

nerves have relaxed and he is comfortable as he lets

exhaustion take him to blissful dreams. There is a tapping on

the edge of his sleep. The tapping is insistent and not

changing. Then he realizes the tapping is real and he sits up

in bed with a start. He heads to his bedroom door and bumps

into Ronald in his night clothes and pistol in hand. Without

saying a word they both head towards the main area of their

home. The tapping is coming from the front door and they

both look at each other and shrug.

"Yes, how can I help you?" Cash says before Ronald

can stop him. Ronald tries to shush him.

There is a muffled voice behind the thick door then a

dog whine. This has them intrigued and they look out of the

side light after turning on the porch light. Harold is standing

there with Cassius and a car in the driveway. Cash opens the

door.

"Harold, do you know what time it is?" Cash says.

"It's 2 am here and you are making me stand out here at this time of night?" He says with a grin. Cassius then sits as he waits for Cash to let them in. Ronald pushes into the doorway as well.

"Who is in the car, Harold?"

"That's my hired driver. The rental car agency in Houston would not give me a vehicle."

"You're quite jovial for this time in the morning, eh?" Ronald steps past Cassius to go get the bags at the edge of the driveway. He pays the driver and a tip from the wallet he grabbed after realizing it was Harold. He brings both bags into the house and closes the door. Harold and Cash have made their way to the kitchen.

"Harold why are you here? We did not know you were coming." Cash says as he grabs the kettle to put tea on. Grabbing a set up of three cups and tea bags, he sets up on the kitchen island. After that he grabs a bowl and gets water for Cassius.

"Tried to call, but you two are hard to pin down. This was not my idea. If I had my druthers I would have stayed in London. This air is humid and the salt is bothering my sinuses. Ool and the crew are a little stressed and homesick."

The kettle is boiling and each set up their tea how they like it. Ronald grabs his tea and Harold's tea then guides him to the living room. After getting him settled in on the couch, he sits in the leather sitting chair to stretch out his long frame. Cash sits in his usual recliner and settles in.

"So what has our benefactors in rattling bits?" Cash asks. He sips his tea and waits for the answer. Harold in turn sips his tea and relaxes.

"They are worried about the team, gear and ammunition. A lot of what they have been doing is on guess work from the Internet and other data. They need to have direction."

"I was worried about that, but moving continents and recruiting is hard. But, we have a good lead on a team so far." Cash says.

"We have two potential candidates that we have here now. It was quite an interview." Ronald says.

"I imagine so with all the antibiotic wafting off you two." He says with a grin. They all chuckle at this.

"Ceramic bullets? Is this your idea?"

"Yes. The issue is that the supply of phez is low. They have enough to build protective suits for a team of four. The remaining is enough to make enough ammunition for a prolonged engagement. It's hard enough and is destructive in knife form. What are your thoughts on it?"

"Thought about it, but I am not a gunsmith so I presented the question to a potential candidate for my Pop's team." Ronald says while his eyes are closed while he stifles a yawn.

"Cash you will have your own team? Never mind. Is it possible for me to stay for the day before I get a hotel?"

"You will not be staying in a hotel. We have a guest room and Cassius is always welcome." Cash says as he gets up and grabs the tea cups. He places them in the dishwasher with the other dishes and starts it. Ronald gets up and grabs the bags and Reginald grabs his elbow as he is guided to the bedroom. Cash lets Cassius out to do his business in the backyard. He soon comes in and pads back to the direction his master has gone.

Chapter 28

Wasting Time

The following morning after breakfast the three make the call to Ool and the crew to set up a meeting for early evening at the old warehouse in Ingleside, TX. All three set up in Cash's office to research information on ceramics and location check for the last team member.

"Looking at this data, he is in Biloxi, MS. His file was not updated after his discharge. It shows that he moves around a lot in the southern United States. There is a probability that we can't go meet him until Wednesday?" Ronald says as he scribbles more notes on his legal pad.

"Wednesday? That is four days away. Burning a lot of time just traveling." Reginald says.

"This is not a phone conversation, but a face to face like gentlemen. So today is Sunday and that is why we are meeting Ool and the flock today. The area near the

warehouse is pretty empty on the weekend."

"Well, son. He has a point. We have been doing a lot

of planning and traveling. Now we have to perform action as

they have paid us mightily and there is nothing to show on

our part. I am going to call Manual Ramirez and pick his brain

over the ceramic issue. You can meet the others on what

they have ready." Cash says as he peers at them over his

reading glasses.

"Well, where does that leave me?" Harold asks.

"Your job is to find a ceramics or tile factory for sale

here in Texas. We do not want to put too much distance

from a potential asset. Also, we have to cultivate other

relationships here in this country. Ronald, what is your Great

Aunt Diane's son's name?"

"Corey Thomas. Why? Pop, why do you want to pull

Manual in so soon?"

"It's about honor, Son. They paid us to help them and we are not making progress. So we have to do better. Corey is family and I believe he is here in the States in...Memphis. I will call Aunt Diane and get his number and get him down here. We need another hand especially for Harold. No offense."

"None taken." Reginald says with a grin as he listens to Cash.

"Each of you has their assignment, so let's break this up. Make your calls and I will make mine.

In short order all go their separate ways. Each find their own space and start making progress. Cash has set up a meeting with Manual for lunch. Then makes the call to Aunt Diane and quickly finds out that Corey is not on the straight and narrow. He slowly convinces her to give him the number and he wants to see for himself. He calls Corey.

"Yes." A female voice says on the other end of the phone.

"Excuse me. Could I speak to Corey Thomas? This is his Cousin Cash." Cash says and waits. There is music in the background and whispers then the phone is passed.

"Cash? I haven't heard from you since I was twelve years old. Is Aunt Diane okay?"

"She is fine son. I am calling you, because my son Ronald and I have moved to Texas."

"Really. What yall doing down there?" Corey says with a heavy southern accent.

"We are running a business and opening others. You busy?"

"Got a couple of thangs going. What you need cousin?"

"I need you in Corpus Christi in two days. Money is at Western Union by the time you tell the young lady goodbye. It is enough to drive down here or take a train. Before you say anything I already know about the prison time and the assault charge. Don't need any problems with you on a plane. Can you handle this?" There is a pause and a door slam.

"She gone and I am on my way after I pack a few things. Thanks Cousin Cash."

Meanwhile on the back patio, Ronald walks around the fountain and makes his calls. After the third number he has success.

"Hello, is this Shawn King?" Ronald asks as he stops to hear the weak connection. The sea breeze off the Gulf of Mexico carries the salt and humidity.

"Yeah, this is him. Who is dis?" the voice on the phone says with a heavy Southern accent.

"This is Ronald Cashmere and I got your number from…" Ronald starts to say before he is interrupted.

"You got my number from the guy at the United Nation Force Command. A buddy of mine gave me the heads up you would be calling. Look whatever you selling, I'm buying." Shawn says and a heavy engine continues to thrum in the background.

"That's good. Where are you so we can meet?"

"Well right now I am on my motorcycle heading through Beaumont."

"Beaumont, Texas?"

"Yes, is there another one I don't know about? A buddy of mine has a boat and I was going fishing. Where do you need me?"

"You will miss your fishing trip, but I have an offer that will make it up to you."

"So where am I headed?"

"Corpus Christi. If you can get here by six, we will have dinner to discuss the possibilities."

"Sure thing. Hey, by the way you talk funny!" Shawn says and hangs up the phone. Ronald shakes his head at this comment. He heads back to his father's office to report what has been discussed. As he gets to the office, Cash is on his way out of the office.

"Pop, I got Shawn on his way. He was already in Texas so he will here by six. How about your endeavors?" He says as he follows him to the living room as Cash is preparing to leave. Glancing to his left he sees Reginald on a braille tablet doing his research.

"Well, your Cousin Corey will be here tomorrow night to give us a hand. Right now I have a lunch meeting with Mr. Ramirez at a place on Alameda. Do you want to attend with me?"

"No sir. I will be around here until the meeting with Ool. Do you want me to wait?"

"No, you handle that one since you will be using the gear. Be careful, because it might hurt." Cash says with a smile and a wink.

Chapter 29

One More Time

Ool, Laz and Prill wait in the warehouse for Ronald to get his suit on. Ronald showed up before them and let everyone in. Before they could explain the suit, Ronald just wanted it to put it on. So they now wait for him to get dressed. The warehouse itself used to be a metal working facility. Perfect environment to test weapons, due to the fact with machinery running noise is blended. All of the three look better than previous days. All there feathers are bright and the salt air is invigorating.

"Do you think it will fit?" Prill says. He asks while he is sitting on one of the leftover benches.

"It will. But, I am more concerned how the test will go. I still feel we need to use physical attack with blows. Using projectiles would not be good at first." Laz says with some discomfort.

There is a clang as the door is opened at the far end of the warehouse. Ronald walks in with the suit on and is absolutely imposing. The change with the plating leaves the suit not overly large. However, the neuro-suit is virtually seamless underneath. There is no stiffness in his movements.

"Okay, you three I somewhat like the suit. You have to allow closure in the front not the back. Also, the crotch area needs more room on both suits. Lastly, by no means do we want a white suit, ever."

They all three surround Ronald and start poking and prodding the suit. This being the first iteration of the suit. Various movements are made to check the flexibility.

"I don't feel stronger in the suit? Also, the helmet with the heads up display, it needs to shorter terms. The terms are too long and I can't pause long enough to read it all."

"Ronald the suit will not enhance your strength. The gravity on our world will give you more strength since the gravity is less then Earth's. It is not weightless mind you, but you will be quite a bit stronger. When we get there we will gauge the strength of you and the team." Laz says.

"However, it is a protective suit, so we must test that premise." Prill says and directs everyone to follow him. They head deeper into the warehouse and enter a door between to sandblast units. When Prill passes them he turns them on and the sound of the fans are loud.

Once they enter the door, Ronald see the heavy panels at the far end and a table set up with weapons. He heads straight to the table and picks up a modified pistol and hefts it.

"This pistol is rather bulky. Is this one of the propellant weapons you designed? Let's give a go." Ronald says and draws back the slide. Laz places his hand on the weapon and lowers it.

"Sorry, Ronald. It will not fire here. We have designed it for our world and the ammunition is not ready. This is to allow you to see that we have been busy as well. There are four of each weapon, assault rifle, pistol, shotgun and shotgun. We also have a razor bow and long rifle." Prill says and lightly strokes the razor bow. This was his creation and can't wait to give a try.

"So we have all the toys and no batteries. So I am all dressed up with nowhere to go. Why am I doing here if we are not going to shoot?" Ronald asks perturbed and then sees the look of all three aliens staring at him.

"What are you three smiling about? By the way it looks pretty bizarre."

"Well since we are here we can check the suit. Now it will hurt." Ool says and waits for the reality to sink in. Ronald shrugs and puts on the helmet.

"Let's get cracking!"

The first blow had no effect or any pain. It was a baseball bat blow to his back and it felt as if a breeze had blown by. The repeated blows to the same area does not bring the desired effect. Blow by blow as the three take turns, no pain is registered by Ronald.

"This suit is amazing! No matter what you are doing I don't feel it." Ronald says from under the helmet. Laz speaks as he is the least tired of the three.

"It must be the velocity. The blunt force is not fast enough to gain enough momentum to register in the neuro-suit. That is a great thing so we know in hand to hand combat the damage will be negated." Prill says as he drops the bat happily.

"So we know that low velocity won't do it…So we have to speed it up. The attack I mean." Ool says and grabs an unmodified assault rifle.

"Take the suit off Ronald. We need you shoot it first. Then once we see it does not penetrate, put the suit back on so we can shoot you." Prill says matter fact. Ronald does what is asked and the suit is hung on the plate wall. Standing in boxers and tank top and unloads the entire clip in the torso and legs of the suit. They inspect the suit and there are no holes in the suit. There are a pile of slugs at the foot of the suit.

"So it seems that it works. Ronald would you mind?"

"Yes, I would. I don't touch any of you enough to shoot me. So the human trial will have to wait. So now I am going to get dressed and hopefully bring someone back I trust to shoot me. By the way how fast can you make three more?"

"The right measurements it can be done in a week. How did it feel?"

"How did what feel?"

235

"Shooting the suit. Seemed fun." Prill says as he continues to stare at the rifle.

"Let's do it one more time." Ronald says and reloads another clip. The Zinghavi have fingers, but their fingers don't fit in the trigger. So living through him, Ronald drops ten successive shots in center mass. Still no hole.

"No penetration, but I wonder what the pain will be underneath?" He wonders aloud as the echo of the shots continue to ring around the room.

Chapter 30

Table for Six

Still riding on the euphoria of the possibilities with just the suit, Ronald tears down Texas 361 to head back to Corpus Christi. The evening sun warms his skin as he heads back for the dinner. In the back of his mind however is getting these three different individuals to sign on with him. Even in their presence of the Zinghavi he still feels like he is dreaming and he has months to get used to the idea. Now getting these four to understand to sign on for a mission will not all hinge on the money. His phone starts ringing through the speakers of the Range Rover.

"Hello."

"Ronald this is Carla. I got a message from your Dad and he says he wants to meet us for dinner."

"Is this us you, Rod and Manual?"

"Of course who else would it be? He asked me to pick the spot. Do we need privacy or not"

"Private would be great. However, add another person to the reservation."

"One more?"

"Understand. Will send the restaurant information shortly. You good?"

"I am great. I will see all of you this evening. Going across the causeway so I have to go." Ronald says then hangs up the line. The skill level of this team will be outstanding once they get there. He makes the call to check on the status of Shawn King.

His dossier shows that Shawn King was a country boy that wanted to serve his country. The funny thing is that Shawn was not just a country boy, but a certified genius. Boredom with school was his downfall. The longer he stayed the more trouble he got into. Building motors and burning up

motors with backroad racing at fifteen years old. His mother

signed him in the military at seventeen since he already

graduated at sixteen years old, but his college test scores

gave him that opportunity. He graduated from University of

Southern Mississippi in three years with a degree in

mechanical engineering. Joined the Navy and became a Seal

at 21 years old. Served two tours and discharged to go to

medical school. After graduating from medical school he

dropped off the grid. Redlining through school, military and

school again, he took his foot off the accelerator.

Slow down he did and just bounced from friend to

friend doing the things that he missed as a boy. Hunting,

fishing and sitting for the last twelve months. Enjoying life for

a little while before he has to step on the accelerator again.

"Shawn? Shawn can you hear me?" Ronald says into

the phone as he is on the Harbor Bridge. Slowed by traffic on the bridge and he decided to check on him. It is the same

sounds as before so he is still riding.

"You told me six?" Shawn says as the roar of the

motor echoing in his earpiece.

"Yes, I said six and I was being courteous and checking

on your status. How far are you?"

"I am close and I will be early. So where are we going

to meet?"

"The Post on Alameda. So how far are you?"

"Crossing the bridge right now."

At the same moment Ronald is wondering if it is his

phone. Then suddenly he realizes the sound is outside the

vehicle to his right. Looking in his rearview mirror there is

Shawn riding on the retaining wall on the side of the bridge.

A chorus of screams and honks follow him as he roars past.

"Well, mate. That was some stunt. Meet you at the restaurant." Ronald says and hangs up his phone.

Rod cleaned up fairly well and decided to hang out at the hangar with Carla till dinner. Sitting in the aircraft office with the air conditioning keeping the warm Texas night at bay. Taking the time to get a haircut with new clothes, he is fairly presentable. His long hair cut above his shoulder and his beard shaved to a goatee. Keeping his wardrobe light and presentable as well. Linen khaki pants with purple V-neck t-shirts and Chuck Taylor's.

"Rod, all that money the Cashmeres gave you and you couldn't buy real shoes?" Carla says as she puts on hoop earrings to finish her ensemble of pale green sundress and wedge open toed sandals.

"So you are wearing that?" Rod says as he peers over the magazine he is reading while sitting on the couch with feet propped on the table. Carla has an apartment on the upper side of the hangar, but kept him down here. The repair

crew were applying that last of the paint to cover the holes in

the plane's skin. After the haircut and shopping then stopping

by his hotel he came here.

"You have a problem with what I have on?" Carla asks

as she turns on a heel to stare at her critic. He then looks

over the magazine again and really looks for the first time.

The dress was quite lovely, but the woman underneath with

her compact build made the dress gorgeous. Her arms in

their definition were truly remarkable.

"Honestly, that is the best you will ever get from me,

Carla Jefferson." Rod drops the magazine and sits up.

"You and I will be on the same team maybe. It all

depends on the deal. Now if the deal is good we are team

members so you are on the same level as Ronald and Manual.

I would never tell them they look nice, so you will always be

treated as an equal."

"Okay, I appreciate that. I don't need your speech. It's fair to ask a question. So now we got things straight, let's get out of here. By the way I know I look good!" Carla says as she puts on her sunglasses and grabs her purse. They both head outside to catch the Uber they had called earlier. Veterans understand that any dinner can turn a little rowdy so it is best not to drive. Rod holds the door open for her and they both get in. They give the address and they head to the meeting that will change their lives.

Manual has put on his best jeans and gaucho shirt with his ropers. His small house is in the same neighborhood he grew up in. He could afford a better house, but his nephews and nieces are important to him. His sisters live three streets over and his mother four houses down. Leaving for the military was stressful especially after his father passed from cancer. Now he has to take care of everyone. The deal Mr. Cashmere offered was more than anything he ever made.

Also, he has the answer to the ceramic bullet. He grabs his

cowboy hat and heads out to dinner.

Chapter 31

One More

The Post is an upscale restaurant for Corpus Christi.

Ronald and Cash arrive together. Rod and Carla arrive soon

after. Manual is waving for them to a side room. Cash, Rod

and Carla head over to meet Manual, but Ronald heads to the

bar. There is a young man at the bar wearing a similar jean

jacket to the news story of a man riding across the bridge

earlier. Ronald comes up next the man as he is drinking

water at a bar. Before he can say anything.

"How you doing, Mr. Cashmere?" He says and turns in

his seat to stand up and stick his hand out in on fluid motion.

Looking at him he looks like a kid, but dimness in his eyes

shows he has seen a lot. He stands at the same height, but is

slender in build. When they shake hands there is a strength

that does not match. After the handshake they both look

each other over. The bar is not that busy, so they are not interrupted. They both smile.

"Mr. King are you hungry? We have a table over there. Join us."

"Thanks, Boss. I could eat a little. You from England or something?"

"Well, yes. Please stop the country bumpkin bit. I have seen your record and you are a genius. Not only a genius, but a doctor as well. That bouncing around was a ploy, you are a graduate of University of South Alabama Medical School."

"Well you are right. But, I am country, it's easier to talk like this, seriously." Shawn then lifts his arm for Ronald to lead the way for introductions. The music is at the right volume where their conversations will be covered by the thump of the Top 40. As they enter the room everyone is still milling around and talking among each other. Ronald makes the introductions and Shawn is soon involved in

conversations and hearing the recap of the Colombia.

"So you stayed there surrounded by the cartels for

one chicken?" Shawn asks as they start taking their seats.

"Yes, he did and that one chicken cost me five grand

to just patch the bullet holes." Carla says as Cash pulls out her

chair. She smiles at the gentleman move and Rod gives her a

look. In turn she shows him the length of her third finger.

The waiter comes in and takes the drink orders for everyone.

A round of waters is soon ordered and appetizers are

ordered. Small talk continues as places where they grew up,

places stationed and plenty of side jokes against the Army,

Marines, Navy and Royal Infantry. Appetizers arrive and they

ask for privacy.

"Alright, lady and gentlemen this is dinner and also a

meeting. I brought you here so we can view the continuity of

the possible teams. My son and I have been sharing

information in a piece meal fashion. Now we want to put all the cards on the table."

"The opportunity is helping a group that has been terrorized internally by their own protectors. They are being abused and even killed for the world to see. An emissary group has been sent to seek help and they chose our firm."

"So this is not some of that Rwanda or Ukrainian issues?" Rod asks as he picks up another wing.

"You are seriously eating chicken? You are not a loyal person, huh?" Shawn asks and the whole table laughs at Rod. He in turn grabs another wing and dips that one too with a smile.

"Okay, everyone let's get back on track. There will be a contract and the pay is substantial. However, once we are there communication will be spotty. So if there is a reason you can't be away on extended time let us know." Ronald says.

"Also, for all the ones interested we will be meeting the envoys in the morning. Carla, is possible for you to get a helicopter that could ferry all of us?" Ronald asks as he sees Manual making eye contact.

"Sure. Where are we flying to?"

"It's local and in the Gulf. It's faster than a bloody boat, there and back. Manual you have something on your mind, mate?"

The table gets quiet and Manual raises his hand like a student in class.

"Sorry, Mr. Cashmere I can't. My family needs me and I can't leave. I am going to leave now, but I have the answer to the ceramic bullet problem." Manual says as he takes off his cowboy hat full of anticipation to tell his idea.

"Ceramic bullets!" Shawn coughs while he is in mid-drink. Shawn's eyes and attention is following everyone else's gaze.

"Stop the smiling and get on with it." Carla says as she pushes her plate of appetizers away.

Manual starts to explain, "Instead of looking at various bullets let's look at the AR-15 round. It weighs fifty-five grains and that is a solid round. Ceramics weigh a lot less, so achieve the weight the round will be large in comparison. So to compensate we could add twenty-two grains of a light metal that is the spine of the round. This will help with lower weight coefficient."

"Okay, what will keep it from shattering going through the barrel grooving?" Ronald asks not to kill the idea, but push it to realistic possibilities.

"Well I remember in a sniper history class that a bullet was wrapped in paper to keep it from being identified. So it will need some kind of coating to keep it together so it will not file down after being discharged." Shawn says as he is on the edge of his seat. At that moment the waitress peeks in.

"You guys ready to order?" She asks and comes in the room with her pad ready.

"Sure. We would like to order and I would like a medium rare steak, sweet potatoes and Brussel sprouts." Carla orders and passes her menu.

"Brussel sprouts? What are you and who are you?" Manual says with a laugh and waits his turn to order. She makes the rounds and everyone has their order is taken.

"Any one a drink?"

All heads shake and all point to get a refill on water. She obliges and heads out to place their orders.

"Now back to what will keep the round together. Anyone else has any ideas for this sticky wicket?" Cash says with glee and rubbing his hands together. He takes off his fedora and d rubs his bald head in anticipation.

"Sorry, I forgot to tell you. The delivery system has less velocity than a typical firearm. These will be internal combustion driven with a lower velocity but sufficient penetration." Ronald says as he sips his water and sees the aggravated looks as the problem just got easier.

"Stop piecing it out! We are so close!" Rod says as everyone has the same thought and he was faster on the response. Ronald holds his hands up in mock surrender.

"Okay, so we have lower velocity so it will not rip it apart." Carla says as she is more engaged.

"Still needs something to hold it together. If you bake it extra hard, will it fail?" Rod says.

They all sit in silence and ponder this problem. Food arrives and there is no conversation as everyone digs into their food. It is quiet and Rod keeps scraping his plate. That

sound has Cash flinching at every stroke. After the last

scrape...

"Mr. Rodrigo would you mind not scraping the plate.

You continue eating this way the glaze will be in your food."

Cash says. Then Manual drops his fork on his plate and grins

for the first time that Cash had ever seen.

Chapter 32

Shock and Awe

The entire crew crawls into the helicopter as Carla and Manual go through the takeoff sequences. As the evening moved on the discussion of the bullet surpassed the conception stage and morphed into trial and error testing in a machine shop. Which ended in complete disaster as none of them knew anything about pottery. This continued to planning of how and whose engagement techniques were better trained by their service. All of this without on drop of alcohol. Adrenalin fall off has the crew tired and groggy.

"Ronald what is my course heading?" Carla asks over the headset as the turbine starts its starting whine.

"Southeast course 18.84, -90.403336 for two hours. Wake me up once we are 45 minutes out so I can direct you to the oil rig."

"There are no active rigs in that direction?"

"I know they are not active, but they are still there."
Ronald answers back and leans back in his seat and closes his
eyes. Rod is sitting to his right and his father and Shawn are
across from him. The Bell helicopter rises smoothly and
makes the trek towards the Gulf avoiding the refineries and
downtown. Riding this high up the city is gorgeous with the
blue water and palm trees. The thump of the blades soon
lulls him to fitful sleep.

Cash watches his son sleep and smiles. Five months
earlier he was sitting in a parking garage and taking quid from
customers. Now he is riding in a helicopter in Texas with a
team to convince to take millions to protect an alien race. His
laugh awakes the whole back of the helicopter since he forgot
to turn off the headset.

"You doing alright, Mr. Cashmere?" Shawn asks as he
leans forward concerned.

"Fine, my boy. Absolutely, great!" Then claps the man on the shoulder and settles back to watch the water.

Ool, Prill and Laz rush in preparing the sitting area for the new team members. The couches were hard to move in and getting the lights right. As the move the tables into place there is a knock on the door.

"Yes, Harold." Ool says as he is trying to catch his breath as they have been rushing since they got the call.

"Mr. Ool, please calm down. These are military veterans and they will see through the pageantry. Set the area and relax so this will go well." Harold says loud and clear through his earpiece.

"Laz, should we bring the weapons up?" Prill asks as he stretches over the table. He is quite winded from taking the stairs up.

"Seriously, we barely are alive from just bringing ourselves up here. If it goes well we can go to the warehouse. I will not kill myself to show off!"

"It's not showing off. It is incentive to get them on our side?"

"Strange to get them on our side is not covered in the currency necessary to make them rich." Laz says as his plumage starts to get more vivid as his anger grows.

"You two better get on the same page. I hear a helicopter coming. Turn down the lights and relax." Harold says from outside.

Carla brings the helicopter in a circling pattern as she verifies that the structure is stable. Manual points and she nods that bringing the helicopter in from the east avoids the wind gusts. As they sit down everyone unloads and secure the helicopter. They all stretch and look at their surroundings.

"This is pretty wicked and I have not seen this much water in a long time." Rod says as he walks to the railing to look down. The breeze is cool and it very quiet. Shawn joins him at the rail and breathes deeply as well.

"You know what I love being out this far?"

"You are allowed to pollute the ocean legally?" Carla says as puts down the last chock. The rig sways gently under their feet and the structure groans quietly.

"There is that Ms. Carla. But, no it is the absence of bugs. Growing up in Mississippi I have been bitten by every kind of insect. Just being out to sea gives me total freedom." Shawn says then opens his fly to pollute the ocean. All the men laugh and Carla shakes her head like she is surrounded by brothers.

"Gentlemen and lady let me show you to our meeting room. Carla would you let me do the honors?" Cash says and sticks out his elbow to escort her to the front. Rod makes the same face and she elbows him in the gut as she passes. He was braced for it with no damage. They start the upward climb to the office facilities.

"This place is pretty clean to be non-operational. Also, there are lights on in there as well." Manual says and points to the structure in front of him and runs his hand along the clean railings. Ronald is bringing up the rear and sees his father entering the offices. He hears the booming voice with the accent and hears the curse from the others as they are surprised.

"Good morning everyone. Especially you me lady. My name is Harold and I am the gatekeeper for this meeting. Please, do me the honor and respect to announce who you are." Reginald says and meets everyone with a handshake and a smile.

"Now the pleasantries are out of the way, I need you to trust me. Please place all of your weapons in the locker on the table. Then all of you take one lock and lock a hasp. This will protect the client and each other." Harold says and stands there in his khaki suit with a light shirt underneath. He cocks his ear as he hears the murmurs.

"Look Ronald and I have been through this. Harold is quite trustworthy and let's comply."

"This allows us to get to the real business at hand. Pony up the weapons please and don't try anything, please." Ronald says and drops in his knife and followed by Cash's knife.

The clatter in the box continues for the next two minutes. After Manual drops his third knife, the box is overflowing with eight guns, nine knives, two ligatures and six dollars in quarter rolls. Harold smiles as he has mentally calculated how much went into the box. He is tipping his head towards the door as everyone gets moving towards the door. He sticks his right hand out and stops Rod before he heads in.

"Mr. Matta, will you please put the knife in your buckle in the box." Harold says with his hand still on Rod's chest.

"Really? I don't have a knife in there." Rod says as he tries to push past. Then the next actions happen in a blur. Rod grabs the wrist of Harold to twist it away. Harold drops to his right knee and shoots his left foot out striking Rod above the joint, which sends Rod stumbling forward surprised. While stumbling his grip is loosened on Harold's wrist. Further pushing his advantage Harold grabs Rod as he falls forward by the buckle and shirt collar then presses him above his head.

"Harold, put him down!" Cash yells and pushes from the door to the side of the big man. There are snickers as Rod screams curses at Harold as he remains eleven feet above the ground.

"Will you put the knife in the box, Sir?" Harold says with no strain in his voice. No one expected this display of strength.

"He will. Right Mr. Matta?" Ronald says as he blocks the door as the floor show continues.

"Fine! Put me down!" Harold squats and lowers Rod to the ground. In turn Rod slips off the belt and places it in the box. He heads to the door behind the others then stops and looks at Harold.

"You move pretty quick for a blind man." Rod says and shakes Harold's hand and they both laugh.

Chapter 33

Three Fingers

The room is entirely different than in London. Due to the location of the oil rig the room is lit from the window. There is a table with seven chairs, seven glasses and a bottle of Blanton's Straight whiskey. The floor is covered in an oriental rug with three leather couches. The group moves into separate areas to examine the surroundings. Ronald and Cash are the first to sit at the table and pour one finger of the whiskey over two ice cubes after opening the bottle.

"Wow, this will be the first drink I have seen you drink Mr. Cashmere?" Manual says as he pulls up a seat next to him. Cash tips the glass towards Manual to show him that he is. Manual holds his hand up backing off. The others migrate to the table and take seats as well. After they are all seated and making small talk, Ronald holds his hand up to get everyone to settle down. He tinkles the ice cubes until all the talk ceases.

"Everyone. We are going to meet the envoy in a few minutes. What I need from you is calm. No matter what you stay calm. You may want to pour a drink?" Ronald says and makes eye contact with every person at the table.

"It's way too early for whiskey." Shawn says as he slouches in his seat and grabs an ice cube from the bucket and rolls it in his hands.

"Well I apologize. We should have brought other beverages, but the whiskey usually helps." Ool says in his tinkling voice as he approaches the group from the rear door. All heads turn and four chair backs hit the floor. There are screams and curses as the new members try to figure out what is happening. Cash and Ronald pour three fingers of whiskey in the team's glasses. Ool stays near the door as the four look to see the Cashmeres unmoving.

"This is a joke, right? This has to be a guy in costume." Rod says and contemplates rushing at Ool to prove it.

Shawn, Manual and Carla gain their composure first. They still don't take their seats and watch as Ool makes his way around the right side of the room and places the table between him and the others. His conical eyes watch each and every one of them. Carla is the first to take a gulp of the fine whiskey and closes her eyes to the burn. Manual in turn does the same and pours another. Shawn on the other hand is grinning from ear to ear. Rod is still on his feet not looking at Ool.

"This is so cool. I never thought I would meet an alien." Shawn says and grabs another ice cube and starts to roll it.

"He is not real! It is a costume! You drag me back to the US for this?" Rod says and starts for the door.

"Come sit down, Rod. Unless you are swimming back, because I had a drink so I can't fly for a while." Carla says and reaches down to pick up the last chair.

"Is it because I look like a chicken?" Ool says and smiles. This statement causes an uproar of laughter from everyone. There is even a howl of laughter from outside of the door from Harold.

"Are you serious!? How does he know about my chicken?" Rod says and heads back to the table as the laughter continues. He slams back the drink and stares at Ool. Then the reality of what he is seeing strikes him. As Ool is standing there, Rod sees the breast feathers moving with each breath. The independent movement of the eyes as he takes in the entire scene in front of him.

"That was conveyed to me in the sense it was. It was what you say quite funny. By no means are we chickens with the only exception being the feathers. If we were any comparison it would be those of your planet's native

penguins."

The collective group stares at Ool in a new light and

there are nods. In their minds it could be a possibility.

"So the mission you have for us is going to another

planet for what?" Rod asks as his muscles twitch from the

overuse of adrenaline in a short period of time.

"It is going to another planet, yes. Then the other

reason is Ool and his species are being persecuted and

slaughtered by another race." Ronald says and sits down his

glass then gets to his feet.

"We are going to give a brief and we are just asking

for the opportunity to get you onboard. You will be

compensated for your time now and well compensated for

the mission. Let us keep open minds and hold all questions to

the end."

Instead of making the presentation on the ship the presentation is made there. All shift to the couches and watch the footage and listen to Laz and Prill. The facial expressions of the group change with each presentation and questions are starting to pile up. Once Laz finishes his description of the planet's atmosphere and food sources, Shawn can no longer contain himself.

"So we see the videos and these Orethians are treating you guys pretty poorly. But, how do we know that you did not hurt them first? Plus, this fight for us is strictly about money and that is putting it plainly "mercenary"." Shawn says and wipes his wet hands on his jeans. He then leans forward with his full attention on Ronald.

"Well, Mr. King as you well know, any military commitment has gray areas. This gray area is helping someone, keep order and make it home safely. Now that is what all of us did for our respective countries." Ronald says and looks at everyone as heads acknowledge this fact.

"Now we are asking if you want to do the same thing, but there is a bigger caveat. You will get paid for the work that you put in. Yes, it is gray, but we have done the gray area before?"

The first to say something after his speech is Carla.

"Ronald that was quite a speech, but this mission is different from everything we have ever done. Even if I gave you a hard yes, what is the plan?"

"The plan is we will go there on a three month deployment initially then take a month off. It will be a two year contract and pay will be substantially more than anything you have ever made." Cash says as he flashes his smile.

"Where will live, can we breathe the air and what will we eat?" Rod asks as he pours another two fingers of whiskey. Now he is just glancing at Ool and not fully staring.

"The living arrangements will be on a ship and a central base. It will give us mobility and stable atmosphere to breathe in. Atmosphere has oxygen, however it is higher than what we are used too. The ship will be retrofitted with freezers and food from here will be stocked. Any more questions?" Ronald says and leans on the arm of the couch.

"Yes. I am not going, but I want to help. So what are you going to do for weapons since the atmosphere has too much oxygen? Any weapon will explode from the chain reaction from the gunpowder." Manual says as checks the brim of his hat.

"You want to see the guns?" Ool asks and drinks the last of his whiskey. He gestures for everyone to follow him to the lower deck. Prill and Laz are standing on the deck next to

a table covered in weapons.

Chapter 34

On the Same Page

All the weapons are picked up and checked by each team member. There are accolades for the precision, but the negative points for the bulkiness is also communicated. Manual is relieved to find that ammunition is not different in size.

"So what is this ceramic? I looked it up and it was a non-lethal substance. It was used as dishes and images. How is that dangerous? Prill asks as the others continue to look at the weapons. For the first time he is not staring at his pad and is looking intently at Manual, who is not touching the weapons.

"Mr. Prill, it is not the material. It is the design of the material. In order to make this work there has to be a nucleus in the shell. Surrounding the ceramic around a metal projectile. Preferably it is the length of the shell to keep the balance. All I try to figure out is what metal to use?" Manual says as he puts down the shell he was using as an illustration.

"There is remaining phez that we can use. It is lightweight and very durable. It is what we are using in the protection suits. Impervious to projectiles and in your suggested application it can be significantly deadly. If the ceramic can hold the projectile under fire?"

"We have a fix for that and that is a glaze. Now what are these suits you are talking about?"

While they were in their deep conversation they did not notice that the others start gathering up to leave. Ronald hangs back and waves to Manual to come meet him near the stairs. As they get to the stairs Ronald pulls both of them to the side.

"I want you to work closely with Laz and Prill here. Get the ammunition developed and Harold will get you the materials besides the phez. Also, have you had any to drink?"

Ronald asks as the rig sways under their feet. The rig groans

and Manual looks down and sees the shadow of something

under the water. Manual nods his head as he tries to see

what it is.

"Do not worry about that there. You will see soon

enough." Prill says and heads up the stairs.

As everyone gathers back in the main room. Ool and

Cash command the room.

"Now we have to get all of us moving so that we get

some things accomplished in the next few weeks.   Ronald, I

want you and your team to sober up and head to the

warehouse on land. Discretion is key so no more flying today.

Manual I need you to go with Harold when you get back.

You, Harold and Corey will coordinate the ceramic issues."

Cash says as walks around the room and picks up the glasses

as he speaks.

"Who is Corey?" Carla asks as opens a bottle of water to hydrate.

"Corey is family and he has a talent of making things happen. Let him drive as well. Best driver you will ever see." Ronald says as he leans back on the couch.

"Why do we need a wheel man?" Rod asks as he gets up to stretch his legs in preparation for the flight back.

"We have no reason for one, but it is a beneficial bonus. Now back to the task. I am turning the rest over to Ool." Cash says and bows then steps to the side.

Ool flattens his kilt and starts his orders for the other half of the team.

"Prill, Laz and I will load the weapons on the ship. Once we are loaded we will meet them at the warehouse. Have the adjustments been made to the suit?"

"Yes, I made them the same day as requested." Laz says.

"That is very good. Bring the suit as well and we will perform a live test on both suits." Ool says with a smile.

"We keep hearing about the suit? What is it?" Shawn asks with excitement. He is the youngest of the group and even in his battle worn mind there is excitement.

"There is no description that would do it justice. Wait and see like Christmas with bullets!" Ronald says and stands up and finishes his water.

All of the team board the helicopter to head back with Manual at the controls. Ool and his team gather up the weapons and head back down to their ship. So the plans are understood and the flight back is lot faster with anticipation. Harold squeezed in for the return flight and is quite happy to be included with the team. It is late afternoon and the streets are packed with people heading to the beach. The helicopter makes westerly track and makes final approach to the airport. Manual makes the landing and all get out. As the blades start to wind down there is another thumping in the air and heading towards them. In the distance a Ford F-350 heading across the tarmac with a security car following close behind. It screeches to a halt and a tall, muscular black man hops out with a dog in tow. The dog runs and jumps up into Harold's arms.

"Uncle Cash! Got your text and everything is lined up." The young man is saying when two security guards are surrounding him with guns drawn.

"Put your hands up! We told you to stop and the authorities have been notified!" The security guard says while sweating through his shirt in the humidity. The young man does not flinch, but smiles and continues to walk forward.

"Corey what did you do? They seem pretty agitated. Ronald says and crosses his arms as he is amused. He knows his cousin and knows that he is not afraid. Inside he just hopes that the guard is not too nervous. The whole team stands there and watches the show.

"Ronald, come on. I came to the gate and they said I couldn't drive over here. Cassius started barking and he seemed anxious. I was worrying about his feelings. Look how happy he is?" Corey says and Cassius even looks at him confused.

"Keep your hands where we can see them!" The other guard screams as Corey wipes the sweat on his face. At this command Corey whirls around and takes off his shirt then throws it in the truck. Standing there with no shirt he turns around to show he has no weapon. Corey is not a small man by any means standing well above 6'3" weighing at least 275 pounds. Intimidation alone might get him shot. On his back is an angel with a flaming sword and three bullet scars on his right shoulder blade.

"Alright gentlemen! That is enough braggadocios behavior from everyone. Ace and Johnny put those guns in the holsters. Corey get in that truck and put your shirt on. This is not the school yard. Call the cops and turn them around. He is with me. Matter of fact all of these gentlemen are with me." Carla says and between both guards. After a pause that makes everyone feel they are making their own decisions. Handshakes and laughter soon follow while introductions are being made.

"So Corey. You remind me of someone who played defensive end for the Cincinnati Bengals?" Rod asks as security leaves.

"That's me. I played end then they wanted me at linebacker, so I balked. Coach got mad so he cut me at halftime. You don't cut me. So for that favor I left our playbook in the Buffalo airport on my way home. Buffalo knocked them out of the playoffs the next week." Corey says

with a laugh and leans against the truck.

"Alright, we are losing daylight. We can catch up later

on at dinner after the shooting party. Corey, you take Harold

and Manual to the new ceramic factory down in Harlingen

and get the deal down. After the deal is done coordinate the

transporting the equipment necessary back here to this

address and set it up." Cash says and hands Harold the card

and he places it in his pocket. Manual and Corey look at him

confused. When Manual is about to speak, Corey holds his

hand up to stop the question. They all load up in the truck

and head out on assignment.

"I have a crew lined up to help us with the work

already." Corey says and heads down Highway 44 to make

their way down south. Cassius hangs his head out of the

window as they all settle in for the drive.

After the first group departs, the remaining group splits up to get changed for the warehouse. They agree to meet in Portland, TX at the Starbucks to make their way to the warehouse. Ronald and Cash head home and the plan is for Shawn and Rod to meet up and ride with Carla. All vehicles roar out of the airport and split in different directions.

Chapter 35

A Little Lower

As planned the two vehicles met up at the designated location. The Cashmeres in their Range Rover and Carla behind the wheel of her Mercedes jeep. After getting their coffee they make the drive to the warehouse through the tiny towns of Gregory and Ingleside. Each person is within their own thoughts, except

"So Carla what do you think?" Shawn asks from the backseat while sipping on an ice water. Shawn knows what he thinks, but he is curious since he technically he is the new guy.

"Well I will let you know, but I realized something and I have a question for you first. On the rig you didn't touch a drink, just play with ice. Then we stop for coffee and you get ice water. Are you sure you were in the military? No caffeine or alcohol, really?" Carla says over the front seat and eyes him in the rearview mirror. There is an awkward silence as Shawn sips his water, but his neck reddens.

"You can check my record if you want too. The reason I don't drink is that the loss is worse when I am drunk, so I have learned to live with it sober. Coffee only in the morning. Not drinking already makes it hard to go to sleep." Shawn mumbles from the back. This draws a sympathetic look from Carla as she realizes she overstepped. Rod shakes his head and swigs his triple espresso shots. Carla decides is best to look past her previous mistake and answers his question.

"The way I feel is that this is exciting and I wonder if we can pull it off. All of us have our own backgrounds and are devastating on our own. Curious how the Cashmeres intend to pull us together?" Carla asks and floats the question for the other two. She keeps the Cashmeres tail lights in front of her and waits. The Mercedes hums along and the leather seats are cool against her skin as the humidity and mosquitos drift past her window.

After finishing his coffee and drinking half of his water, Rod is ready to answer.

"I like the old man. He is pretty tough old bird. Ronald is okay too, but he is British and they move so methodically in the field. We are looking at a four man team in an unknown environment, untested weapons and eating freeze dried foods for three months. It's doable." Rod says and then spits out of the window, which lands on the back window. Carla looks at him.

"You will be cleaning that up when we stop. If not I will hurt you and leave you out here." Carla says and Shawn laughs in the back then hands Rod a napkin. While Rod looks back forward he sees the Rover pulling inside an automatic gate to a warehouse compound. They follow them to the right to the back warehouse. Both vehicles are parked and they all get out. The warehouse is well lit and machinery can

be heard running inside. They get to the entrance and Ronald

puts in a code and does a retinal scan. There is whisk and a

click then the door is opened and the noise is even louder.

Ronald holds the door and Cash leads them into the

warehouse and the door closes. The lathes are turning,

sandblaster tanks are circulating and the air conditioner is

keeping the entire space cold. Due to the noise conversation

is near impossible. As an entourage they move deeper.

Going through the next door all the noise stops.

"Wow! This is a lot better. Why are we in this noisy

warehouse? Hey wait a minute I like the soundproofing." Rod

says as he takes in the entire vastness of the warehouse

section. There are soundproofing pads over the three walls

and last wall is all metal plates. Plates have bullet damage

and to their right sitting on benches are the three

Zinghavians.

"How are these guys traveling around? I know they are not driving on the streets." Shawn says as he heads straight for them.

"You guys have a transporter or something to beat us places?" Shawn says half joking and the other half curious.

"We have a ship. It is submersible as well so we pilot here and enter through the cove in the back." Laz says so matter of fact that Shawn thinks he is joking. Carla hears the word ship and gets closer.

"You have a ship? Can I see it?"

Ronald calls the room to attention and focus on the tables in front of them.

"Everyone we are here to show you our gear and get some gunpowder in the air." Ronald says and grabs the suits from the table and walks and hangs them on the plated wall. They all look at the suit as it hangs. Without warning Ronald grabs an AR-15 and starts shooting with no warning. It has a

suppressor so the absence of noise does not match the

movement of the suit as it is peppered center mass. There is

collective gasp after the click of the trigger and the suit still

was in one piece.

"You have got to be kidding me? I want a turn. Not

enough punch." Rod growls and puts in ear protection and

everyone scrambles to do the same. The Mossberg 12 gauge

has the punch especially with slugs not buckshot. Six slugs

impact the suit in the same location with the suit no worse

for wear. As the echoes die out they all remove their hearing

protection and jog over to the suit. All hands touch the suit

and there is no damage. There is no heat or no fraying of the

material.

"What is this made of? I have seen all types of gear,

but never this!" Rod says in amazement.

"Do we have anything, something with more power over there? I think I can damage it. How about a 50 caliber?" Shawn says as his eyes dance with the opportunity to destroy something. Cash laughs and grabs Shawn by his shoulders before he bolts. Laz and Prill block the table as well.

"It is called phez and it is impervious to projectile, heat and blunt force. It is one of the most durable materials on our planet. So using it as a protection suit makes sense." Laz says as he walks closer and uses his telescopic eye on Shawn who is still analyzing possibilities.

"It protects you, but does it have any radioactive properties? Carla asks and Rod takes a step back.

"No, it has none. The physical force from any outside force dissipates over the suit to prevent degradation. We have tested it with blunt force with the neuro suit." Laz begins and is cut off.

"Neuro suit? What is it and where is it?" Carla asks and sees the Cashmeres off to the side watching all of the questions. This aggravates her more as they are not helping. But, smiles as they are having fun.

"This is the neuro suit and it will transmit pain to the wearer. The reason being is that with the phez you will not feel anything and that could be detrimental. If you are taking fire, you will not know where it is coming from. This could very well lead to death if not aware." Prill says matter a fact as the suit is being looked at by everyone.

"We have tested the neuro suit on Ronald and there was no registered pain with blunt force using a bat. However, he would not let us shoot him. For us to understand the limits, Ronald could you get dressed please?" Laz asks and points to the door.

"Did you let the crotch out, first? Also, did you lose the zipper? Unless the zipper is phez it is a weak spot." Ronald asks as he hands his watch and chain to his Dad.

"Yes to the crotch and the zipper is still in the back. We will remove it and find a better closure. Good news though, Harold bought soft tip bullets so it may not be that bad?" Prill says.

"You let a blind man buy bullets? That had to be crazy exchange. I need some bullets. Can't you see I'm blind? Here is my list." Shawn says and everyone starts laughing as Ronald laughs himself and leaves to get dressed. While he is gone the others take the time to focus on their newest member, Shawn.

"So Shawn I know Ronald knows you and has seen your jacket. So what is the background and specialty? We have the time and you are different." Rod says as he keeps his eyes locked on Shawn. Cash wants to intervene, but he understands this is not his place as he is not a veteran.

"Well Senor Matta…I am a Navy Seal veteran and I don't like to advertise. I joined and seventeen years old and did two enlistments as a corpsmen. Finished my undergrad in mechanical engineering before I got out. Fell off into medical school and learned to fix people without bullets flying. I have been bouncing around the last two years as a fill in trauma surgeon. Plus, I can pick off a target at more than a mile. Steady hands for killing and fixing. You good?" Shawn says without eyes wavering. There is a deadly cool in him they had never seen to this point. There is a creak and Ronald is back. Cash emits a low whistle.

"So this the suit stuffed?" Rod says and everyone giggles. Ronald has on the suit and it has the look of a bobsled suit, but significantly bulkier. Every inch is covered with underlying padding, the neuro suit. The boots and gloves match the suit and as he walks towards them the colors continue to change.

"Why does the suit keep on changing colors?" Carla says as she walks towards Ronald and touches the suit. It is cool to the touch and there is an excitement of the unknown as she visualizes her own suit.

"So Ronald do you trust anyone in the room, now?" Ool asks as he smiles his disarming smile. Ronald looks around the room and points at Carla. He then places his helmet on his head and heads towards the plated wall. Ool with the signal has loaded Glock 9mm with soft tip bullets and hands the gun to Carla.

"Shoot him, please. Concentrate the shots..." Ool begins to say, but Carla starts shooting. Four successive shots leave everyone in shock as the suddenness caught them unprepared. Cash is horrified when the bullets slam into Ronald who in turn does not flinch. Carla hands the gun back to Ool and all walk forward to check the damage. Ronald is removing his helmet.

"That was quite exhilarating." Ronald says with a smile and smooths his hand over his chest. There is no damage to his torso.

"However, the most horrifying part is that with the helmet display you can see the bullets. It shows the trajectory and speed so literally you see it coming. When they impacted the suit I felt a tingle on the first impact then with each other one."

"A tingle? So what would happen if the same spot is hit over and over again?" Cash says as the relief is apparent on his face.

"Only way to find out. I got it." Shawn says and grabs the gun from Ool. All came back to the firing line and the shots start flying. Shawn pumps five shots in precise and methodic squeezes on the trigger. Ronald staggers and drops to a knee. Cash shouts and everyone runs to check on

Ronald. He stands up before they get there and takes his

helmet off. He is rubbing his sternum and there is evident

pain of his face.

"Ronald let's take off the top and take a look." Shawn

says in his doctor voice. They peel the top off and remove

the neuro suit as well. On his sternum above the xyphoid

process there is a slight bruise.

"The only way I can describe it as a tingle followed by

punch and lastly a hammer. It goes from the point of impact

and radiates across my whole chest. Now if we are taking fire

it will let us know where it is coming from. However, we

can't fall into thinking we are invulnerable. The neuro suit

helps keep us honest." Ronald says and gets the nod of

approval from Laz and Prill.

"Also, next time aim a little lower it really hurts."

Ronald says with a smile.

Part 3

Chapter 36

Crack On

It took exactly four weeks for all things to get in order.
Manual, Harold and Corey were successful in obtaining the
ceramic shop and the bullet process was refined. Due to the
time constraints the manufacturing remained in the valley
and Manual handled the transport. The phez was split and
refined into pins that was surrounded by ceramic. Success
was lowering the velocity and widening the weapon barrel
borings. Every team member had their weapons sized to
them as well as their suits. Tomorrow is departure day and
last minute details are being handled.

A new ship was brought by Slill and outfitted with
freezers and stocked with beef, venison, pork and fish.
Vegetables and fruit jarred and canned. Growing plants will
be brought later. Two reverse osmosis plants are brought

along with at least two months of drinking water. Shower tanks have been brought along as well until a forward base can be established. The newer ship is three times larger than the ship Ool had traveled on. The Zinghavian ship is round in circumference and has the color changing abilities such as the suits. It is powered by three fusion reactors that give it a limitless power source. Storage areas are below deck of the living quarters, training facility and labs. The crews are ready to head back home and the other to a new adventure.

Shawn packs his remaining bag of clothes and already has his books stored. The medical bay on the ship is fully stocked and he has two med packs on standby within his own gear. Storing his motorcycle in the hangar is the only possession he is leaving behind. He gets all his gear down to the hotel lobby and loads it all in Corey's truck. They sit and wait for Rod to head down as well.

Shutting down the satellite feed that he had been using to check on his farm in Colombia. There are no occupants at his farm now, it is overgrown. Hopefully on his return trip he can head down for a couple of weeks. All of this has been sort of surreal, but the reality of what they are about to do has not sunk in. He is grabbing his bags and his cellphone chirps a message, which reads "Hurry Up!" from Shawn. Rod shrugs and heads down and loads up.

"Alright, fellas. What do you want to eat before heading out?" Corey asks as he pulls into traffic. They both know Corey does not know where they are headed or who they are working with. Cash decided to keep it to just the privy few that are on the team, Harold and Manual. He oversees the ceramic factory and a couple of other enterprises that will be up and running by the time they get back.

"I want some tacos and a lemonade." Shawn says from the passenger seat. He has the window down and the weather is cool for October.

"Whataburger for me." Rod says from the backseat.

"Got it." Corey says and wheels the truck down Ayers Street. Makes the first stop at the Taqueria near the college. Makes the left turn and turns left on Baldwin then stops at the Whataburger. He soon makes his way to the Harbor Bridge towards the warehouse staging area. All of the crew is meeting there and will take off for their mission at two am. Last minute stores and ammunition load out will take them up till that time.

"Manual, look at the maintenance records and make sure Wanda stays on schedule. Also, whatever travel Cash comes up with, he can rent a plane for overseas travel." Carla who has been leaving instructions and pointers for Manual for weeks. Manual understanding her stress has just been listening. He nods as she continues to pack her remaining

gear. Her gear is mostly workout clothes and flight suits.

"Why are you taking flight suits? What are you going

to fly?" Manual asks as he starts grabbing her bags.

"The ship! I will be flying the ship and I let them know

that already." Carla says with surprise in her voice. She grabs

her backpack and follows Manual to his truck. After the bags

are loaded, she turns back to Wanda and touches her nose.

Plants a kiss and comes and gets in the passenger seat. They

head out of the airport and wave at the guards on their way

to the warehouse.

"You hungry?" Manual asks before the head

downtown.

"Naw, I ate earlier. You good with me leaving?"

"Sure. You coming back anyway." Manual says with a smile and then cranks up the radio. They drive to the warehouse with no words spoken.

Ronald and Cash sit in the warehouse and are having tea. Cash is in a somber mood as his only son is heading off to space. Sitting there in slacks, drivers and loose fitting sweater. He is wearing a driver hat over his bald head. Ronald is sitting across from his father at the card table. Dressed in joggers, shoes and long sleeve t-shirt. He too is sad as he looks at the furrowed brow of his father. His father is thinking of his mother and doesn't want him to be with her.

"Pop, it will be fine. This first one will be the most difficult and I will be back soon. You need to concentrate on what is next to expand the business."

"Well I have been thinking about that and about you. Son, I do not want you to go. There are so many things that could go wrong." Cash says as he pulls of his hat and wrings it between both hands.

"Pop, we have been over this. I will be back. Now the business?"

"Well, there is a security options that could be a possibility. It is working for non-criminals for a contract. There is also real estate. The garage back in London is up and running. I was thinking if we could get a few of those, money in construction and maintenance will be lovely."

Ronald sips his tea and listens to his father in this quiet moment. The others would be there shortly.

"Could you do me a favor, Pop? Please, do not go to London without security. The Savage lass may be looking for us still."

"Son, it has been nine months? Do you really think we are still being hunted?"

"It is possible. Time to wrap up. I hear the crew

coming in."

Chapter 36

Too Fast

Benefits of a larger ship means everyone has their

own space. Carla, Rod and Shawn are getting settled in their

cabins, Ronald is touring the ship behind Slill. This is the first

time Ronald has spent any time with Slill.

"Now Ronald this is my ship and you are visitors.

What I say you listen. Now this is the way to the bridge, so

you get all of your crew up here. You have twenty slips, I

mean minutes." Slill barks out and strides away from Ronald.

The hallway is lit from lighting below the deck that reflects

from the sides. Slill and his gray feathers are dull on the

edges.

"Yes Sir Mr. Slill." Ronald says and smiles with a salute

to the receding figure. Ronald jogs off laughing towards the

cabin. The joy and sensation of what is to come has the

excitement coming in waves. He reaches the cabins and

gathers the others. They all in turn run down the hallway towards the bridge. Once they arrive and the door parts open. They are too stunned to move. The bridge is immaculate. It is sleek in its design with stations to the side for different functions. Crew seats have been installed to accommodate their larger frames. Looking at the navigational controls there is no stick just a pad. There is a whine that is felt beneath their feet. Slill is at the controls throttling a pad in connection with the whine that is building in volume.

"Now. All of you have to listen before we leave. This ship is not like your Earth propulsion rockets. It is fusion driven and air driven for stability. So there are no suits and there will be gravity. I do not know how humans will respond to the travel. Please secure your bodies in the seats. Laz and Prill will monitor you as we travel. Please put these monitors on your wrists." Slill states and each member of the team is handed a metal bracelet with two leads. As they are put on the leads are connected by adhesive on the wrist. Their pictures and vitals appears on the screens left and right.

"Well these are really helpful. Do we wear them all the time or just for travel? If not it will help me monitor the data after each mission." Shawn says as he leans over the console and sees all the important data; pulse, respirations, heartbeat and exertion level.

"These are implanted in the suits already. These are for comfort level for the length of travel. I will explain the length of the trip once we are in space. Seats." Slill says sternly and heads towards his seat at the console. When he fastening his belts, everyone realizes they are leaving. They all scramble for the seats and strap in. Ool, Laz and Prill are at their consoles as well. The whine of the pumps are steady and the ship starts to move through the cove. At this time of evening the water is dark and bubbles roll over the forward screen.

"Everyone, the ship is running on water right now. There are four pumps that draw water and filter it through jets to control thrust and direction. Once we get out to the rig area we will convert to our vertical ascent." Laz says. The momentum of travel is barely felt in their seats.

"Ronald, this is amazing. We have to traveling at least twenty knots by now. I barely feel any movement." Carla says as she is sitting across the aisle from Ronald with Shawn and Rod behind them.

Meanwhile on the pier, Cash is alone with his tears as they head off to the unknown. He waits until he sees the imperceptible wake get to a point it is no longer visible. He wipes his eyes with his handkerchief and heads back to the warehouse to oversee the storage. As he makes his way through the warehouse, he locks every door behind him.

Once he gets to the front bay, he sees the Manual and Corey talking by the trucks.

"They are on their way. Manual we have a meeting in Florida in two days, is Wanda ready to go?"

"Depends Mr. Cashmere. Is it a meeting or a welcoming party meeting?" Manuals says with a smile.

"Working with me I will do my best is to have a meeting. Welcoming parties are Ronald's cup of tea." Cash says with a laugh and shakes Manual's hand.

"Corey you are coming as well. However, I want you to stay in Portland tonight. I am leaving right now and Manual, you follow an hour from now. We will keep discretion in our visibility.

After an hour of travel and everyone has gotten with the ride. Slill changes tactics. He cuts the rear jets and redirects the jets under the ships body. They rise steadily until they break the surface. Their ears pop with the depth change.

"Hey, next time warn us on maneuvers." Rod groans sleepily from his seat. Everyone else is awake and anxious for what's next.

"Understand. Next maneuver!" Slill barks over his shoulder. The whine of the pumps lessen then there is a rumble that rattles the dog tags on their boots. Without warning there is a moment of weightlessness and the entire cabin is floating. Fusion generators engage and they rocket straight up. There is a howl from Carla as her speed fix is met. Traveling straight up the pressure on them is gradual the higher they rise.

"The reason we are not being crushed is that the artificial gravity is being adjusted as thrust and altitude meet certain markers. That is why are your vitals are stable except

Mr. Matta." Prill says and everyone looks at Rod as he grips his seat armrests in a white knuckle grip.

"You will have to breathe soon." Shawn says with a laugh. Everyone joins him in laughter and then as the clouds fall away there is silence. The first sight they see is the moon as they come out of the atmosphere on the opposite side of Earth. There are no words to describe the beauty of what is before them. The moon is the closest object to them, but the majestic beauty of the solar system leaves them speechless. Satellites and other smaller debris float in a synchronous movement as Earth and its cloud masses are beneath them. They hover in place as they Slill puts in his headings.

"What do you do for coordinates?" Carla asks as she remains in awe as satellites orbit around them.

"Coordinates are too small. Here there is no North or South, just headings. We have two weeks of travel ahead of us. Right now we are headed to Q7B wormhole past Mars.

Stay in your seats until we achieve .25 light speed." Slill says and slides the acceleration bar forward. There is a sensation of being lightheaded and all of the human passengers blackout for an instance. As the acceleration continues the darkness continues to hold them all. Slill and Laz see all of the alarms as they all lose consciousness at once. However, when the ship hits the desired speed they all awake with a start.

"What happened?" Ronald asks groggily.

"Why do my teeth feel numb?" Shawn asks as he lazily licks his lips to make sure he can.

There are the clicks of buttons and Prill answers as Ool grabs bottles of water from a container. He hands one to each person.

"There is a transition from linear speed to sub-light. That transition is not translated by the human mind. The brain waves that show consciousness are nullified. The mind cannot exist in different planes of speed. We have to develop

a solution to mitigate that issue." Laz says.

Chapter 37

Slips

After achieving that speed Slill sits at the controls and

takes the ship deftly around spaced debris and other celestial

bodies. The deftness of movement is aided by forward sonar

that foreshadows issue a range display. Running at .25 light

speed the distance to Mars is starting to decrease. The team

heads back to their cabins to grab something to eat and use

the facilities.

Carla is the first one back to the bridge and

approaches Slill at the controls. She watches while everyone

is milling around. Controlling the ship is an embedded

toggling stick. The movement of the stick is not center point

connected, it is a sliding point for hard and easy turns. It also controls elevation and dives. Speed is controlled by touch

control slider. The slider is only a quarter of the way up.

"Have you figured it out yet?" Ool asks from behind

her. She is not surprised and shakes her head.

"Not yet." Carla answers. She is mimicking the hand

movements Slill is performing.

"Well, Carla. Let me get the ship past the worm hole

and when we get to the next galaxy we have seven days of

travel. I will let you fly there. Now you can watch." Slill says

in his continuous no nonsense to tone. However, there is a

twitch of a smile on his stoic lips.

After getting back to Corpus, Cash wrapped up some

email inquiries. The meeting being scheduled for Wednesday

gave him a day to at least sulk around the empty house.

Harold and Cassius were back in London after getting the

remaining ammunition created. As for the ceramic plant they

would continue to work on a line developed by a local artist.

Fairly good work and keeping the staff gainfully employed allows more diversity. Cash understands that the company is making a lot of money from one employer. That type of money though calls a lot of attention to one's self, so the water has to be muddier. Wednesday's meeting is breaking up a coup from a rival competitor that has turned more into an elimination campaign. It's an inside job and they are on a mole hunt. The phone rings and its Corey.

"Yes, Corey." Cash asks as he goes to his wardrobe to grab an ascot he intended to wear for the meeting. Americans do not understand the deftness and style of an ascot he thinks to himself.

"Uncle Cash, how long are we going to be in Florida?" Corey says with some kind of game going on in the background. Cash offered Corey to stay at the house with him, but Corey decided he needed his own space. In the long run it was the right decision.

"The meeting is Wednesday and want to start the assignment as soon as possible. So it depends how long it takes us to get the assignment completed. Is there an issue for you being gone for a period of time?"

"Nothing like that Uncle Cash. It's that we short on bodies. Me, Manual and you are not enough."

"Corey you mean Manual, you and I, never mind. I have some contacts that Ronald left in the area."

"Come on Uncle Cash, no English lessons right now. Well I figured. But, anyway I have some people that need some work too. What do you think?" Corey says and there is silence on the other end. Cash contemplates this request and does not want to discourage his ambition. He refused to dictate every decision.

"Have them meet us for dinner Wednesday. Since you are vouching for their worthiness, I assume they are bit cheeky?"

"They are and you will appreciate them. Talk to you later." Corey says and hangs up.

Rod has taken the last hour in the makeshift gym in the hangar area. He puts himself through a series of jumping rope and shadow boxing to clear not only his mind but get his legs use to the artificial gravity. When he is jumping rope there is hesitation when bringing his feet off the ground. This took something to get used to and he soon has it down pat. Pushing himself for thirty minutes and give time to shower before the next jump.

Shawn has taken his time to review the vitals from when they all went unconscious. The data shows there was a spike in melatonin during the shift in speed. The problem is to offset the dump of the hormone to stay conscious. Spending the short time he has left he reviews possible countermeasures to stay conscious. Trying to find a possible protection to the pineal gland. While he is thinking about this there lights in the cabin start blinking.

"Crap, it must be time for the next jump!" Shawn yells and drops his medical journal and heads for the bridge. On his way out of the room he runs into Ronald and Rod. He falls in line behind him as the jog the remaining way to the bridge. Entering the bridge everyone is in their same seats. Carla already is strapped in.

"Now this is a longer jump and we saw what happened in just the speed transition. This time we are entering a wormhole and this is a first as well, so our apologies for any discomfort. Has everyone eaten? If not that may be a great decision." Prill says and engines hit their crescendo. Ronald is speechless as the ship rounds the edge of Mars. The colors are too spectacular to even describe with so many variances that are unexplainable. However, when the ship starts to accelerate a black spot in a void starts to

316

glow in an emerald shimmer. As the ship slips into the green shimmer, Ronald sees his hand disembody and all those around them experience the same phenomenon. There is a shudder and pressure behind his eyes that causes him to scream in agony then darkness.

The flight from Texas to Florida was uneventful and they are on their way to a private airport near Tallahassee. Manual is an excellent pilot and does not make the acrobatic maneuvers he was braced for after Carla. His co-pilot is a young man named Robert Currie, a young man from Chicago. He and Corey have the entire cabin to themselves. Corey has been asleep since the engines started and has not moved since. Cash enjoys his peace and grips his son's European phone in his hand. He missed him so much.

"We are close to landing, you may want to call ahead to verify transportation?" Manual says over his shoulder.

Cash looks out of the opposite window and sees the

sun setting. Looking to his left he sees the beaches below

and has a thought.

"Why am I calling to check on transportation?" Cash

says back to Manual while he digs in his pocket for his phone.

"Well, Mr. Cash I am trying to land a plane up here.

Do you really want Corey to do it?" The plane starts its final

approach and the runway is the next stop. Cash calls and two

SUV trucks are waiting outside the terminal. While on the

phone Corey finally wakes up as the engine start winding

down. He wipes his massive hands over his eyes.

"Man, we already here? I need more sleep."

Chapter 38

The Squeeze

Ronald is continuing to be squeezed as he is escaping the flooding of the green river. As he keeps climbing the tree the river is a snake encircling his chest and squeezes his lungs to the point he strikes it over and over. The blows are solid and the beast does not move then suddenly it's gone. Ronald inhales deeply and realizes he is still seated. There is a flurry of activity as alarms are wailing as all of the team's vitals are off the chart. Prill, Laz and Ool are hovering over them and each team member is in a state of confusion and distress. As his eyes adjust the lights in the tunnel they are going through is pulsating and curving. There are objects that his mind cannot decide if they are real or alive. Ool waves his hand and gets his attention.

"Yes, Ool. What is wrong with us?" Ronald says over a thick tongue with a metallic taste in his mouth. Apparently, he had bitten his cheek during the entrance in the wormhole.

"We are so sorry. We had no idea this would happen. The dimensional shift caused a disruption to your nervous systems. Slill had to press us further in faster than usual. Risking a drop out and then reattempting would be further stressful. So we pressed and the full dimensional shift got stability to your systems. Unfortunately, we have more jumps. How many Slill?"

"We have another six jumps not including light speed in between. It would be much easier if we put them down." Slill says with no expression.

"What do you mean put down?" Rod says as he struggles to his feet ready for a fight. He is unsteady of his feet, but fully capable of damaging anyone.

"I believe he means for us to sleep during those times. I prefer not to sleep a lot, but I prefer that to doing this over and over again." Shawn moans as he holds his head between his legs. There is a burp, but no further bodily activities.

"Also, maybe if we can float through it?" Carla says as she is up on her own feet faster than everyone else.

"What do you mean "float" through it?" Ool asks intrigued.

"This is a physics understanding that I have from just flying jets. As pilots we undergo gravitational forces when we maneuver. The forces are thrust going forward and gravity pulling us back. Is it possible to shut down the artificial gravity prior to the jumps so that one of the forces is eliminated?" Carla asks as she opens her bottle of water and looks expectantly at Ool.

"That is plausible and possible. However, if does not work. Short term sleep is the next step. Without these jumps

the time to get to our planet is not in our lifespan capacities."
Prill says as he types away at the controls.

"We can do it. I have enough supplies to get us into short term comas where the reactions are not as violent. But, one of us will have to monitor the others during the jumps. Maybe, a light sedative will lessen the pain on who is awake. Rotating the pain is only fair."

Manual and Corey are loading the luggage into the first SUV while Cash makes the final contact prior to the meeting. Robert the new pilot is securing the plane for storage as they will not be leaving for a few days. The plan is that Cash, Manual and Corey will take one of the trucks and Robert will be on standby with the other. If necessary they will bring him in on a peripheral role. He is a veteran like the rest from the US Navy as well.

"Mr. Cashmere. There is a better way to make things easier." Robert says as he walks past with the last of the

322

wheel chocks. He is built like a striker. Shorter in stature

than the others and slender. However, he moves with such

quickness that betrays an innate strength and power.

"What do you mean Mr. Currie?" Cash asks as he

stares at his phone with his reading glasses. He is sitting on

the bench outside of the hangar and trying to enjoy the cool

breeze that is hard to find in the Florida humidity. In his

traditional slacks and linen shirt, Cash is stylish and proper at

all times.

Robert slings the chocks into place and punctuates

placement with a swift kick. His flight suit is tied around his

waist due to the heat. In his t-shirt Cash sees the tattoos

running down both arms and his neck. The tattoos are of

crosses and portraits of what he can see. He turns back and

looks Cash in the eye.

"You need a quartermaster. Let them take care of all

of the logistics of travel, lodging and transportation. It allows you to worry about the jobs and better organization. Also, I

don't want the job." Robert says matter of fact manner. His

accent or his mannerisms are not southern.

"Quartermaster. Mr. Currie where are you from if you

do not mind?" Cash asks as he puts his phone down as the

young man has his full attention.

"Sir. I am from Detroit. Joined the Navy right out of

college. Graduated from University of Michigan with a

degree in Electrical Engineering." Robert says in the same

tone.

"Must been an exceptional soccer player. Striker or

center back?" Cash asks just to test his own observation. A

smile creeps across the stoic man. The others come from the

truck as they are ready to go.

"That's pretty good. Played midfield all sides. Striker

every once in a while. Liked playing defense too much. Tried

a couple of years overseas, but my ankle injuries slowed me

down. Learned how to fly after I joined the Navy. Did my time and private contract flying now."

"Love the idea of a quartermaster. I will think about it." Cash says and gets to his feet and heads to the truck. Manual gives last minute instructions to Robert and per diem money. He meets Corey and Cash in the truck with Corey behind the wheel.

"Take us to the hotel first so we can get changed for the meeting. Manual you will be with me and Corey stay behind the wheel when we head to our meeting." Cash says as they pull off.

Chapter 39

Packing a Punch

Three days later the crew has gotten use to the travel through the worm hole. Space travel is not a straight line and there are substantial curves and drops as they traverse their new path. Sickness and equilibrium issues passed the longer they were into the journey. Setting up a routine also kept their minds from straying to panic as they get further and further from their own universe. The structure of the day was around regular meals together, training, shooting and learning.

In the storage hold Prill and Laz are finishing the shooting gallery to test fire the rounds. The attempt was tried on Earth and the gravity continued to affect the accuracy and damage capabilities of the rounds. Prevention of possible damage is being eliminated by housing the target within gel filled frames to absorb the shells. It also allows an analysis of the shell and its deployment. Everyone is itching

to give it a try and all are there with exception of Slill.

Someone has to fly.

"Well here we go. Everyone lines up and the selection

of firearms will be pistol, AR, long rifle and the new shotgun.

Before anyone says anything else, I am shooting the shotgun.

Firing sequence will be Rod, Carla and Shawn." Ronald says

and smiles. He puts on his shooting glasses and before the

earplugs go in he is interrupted.

"Hold on. Why do I only get the pistol? This is not

right. You drag us on the job to be squeezed by the universe

like oranges! Then you only let me shoot a pistol?" Rod yells

at everyone. He is truly upset and all people involved laugh

including the Zinghavians. After receiving his answer, he puts

on his glasses and grabs the pistol.

"How do you want the shots?" Rod grumbles.

"Straight line, direction is your choice." Ronald says with a smile. Rod shoots an aggressive line fairly straight. The impact of each shell is muted on the impact and it absorbed in the gel. Once the slide is locked back and the range is safe. They all walk across the storage unit to see the damage. The gel blocks are set as blocks of ice and are set in frames. Laz is pulls back the canvas from the side to check the damage. All heads lean in. The shell entered the gel block and the ceramic explodes out as a flower within the gel. The pin sized phez has cut through the gel and leaves a wobbled pattern in a downward motion.

"So it seems we have spinners. This pattern is with every shot. These are going to be nasty! I wonder once we get one of them, we map out their organs we can calculate trajectories." Shawn says. The next two weapons under the hands of Carla and Shawn. The same result with the other weapon should produce more increased damage and same wobble pattern.

"Carla, you are next. Same pattern in three round bursts. I am curious about the pattern and how it will shift?" Ronald says and heads back to the firing line. The others follow and Carla pumps three short bursts in a similar patterns to Rod's although lower. At the click of the slide they head back again. The gel blocks are further shredded as the pins have crossed each other on impact leaving spider webs of damage. Porcelain fragments and the flowered patterns are beautiful in their suspension. Looking past that then the spider webs of possible destruction is awe inducing.

Cash enjoyed Florida a little bit more in South Texas. The Lone Star state has a certain swagger that his English bred spirit sometimes he could not understand. Sitting in the hotel lobby watching people go by. There are the couples on honeymoons, families on vacation and then there is Manual and Corey. They head towards him as they leave the

elevator. Manual is dressed in the suit he got him, navy blue

with light grey stripe. Finally, cutting his hair and shaving

gives him a different appearance. The scarring on his face

was hidden by the different set of clothing.

Corey on the other hand is wearing khakis and a

button down shirt. Cash chose this, because Corey is driving.

However, as massive as he is even in a suit he would stick out.

As they get closer Corey is looking past him with a smile.

Cash turns in his seat to see three women coming in. They

are all of Hispanic descent and vastly different. Cash

instinctively stands to his feet and buttons up his own slate

grey suit then picks up matching fedora. Manual stops next

to him as Corey passes them both and heads straight for the

trio of women. They all smile then the one in front with teal

sundress slaps Corey, hard. Cash and Manual say nothing,

but smirk.

"You call me after leaving my apartment in the middle of the night three years ago! The nerve of you! I don't care what you want!" The woman in teal screams at the top of her lungs. Her two friends laugh and direct her to the elevators. Corey rubs his cheek and displays numbers; 324 and pushes through the hotel lobby doors. Cash and Manual head for the stairs two minutes apart towards the third floor.

Prill has cut the artificial gravity as they prepare to drop from the wormhole to enter the next. Wormholes are not connected as one would think. Dropping out and navigating to the next could be tedious. The entire crew is strapped in a seat and their limbs are floating as if they are in a swimming pool. Each person has an IV started in their right arms. There is syringe in each of their hands with a dose of midazolam. It is fast acting and does not leave the hangover effect.

"Remember if the same thing happens push the syringe. It will burn and you will be out. I will not push mine. But, if I start getting squeezed like a tick on a dog, Ool knock me out." Shawn says with that cocky lopsided grin that has started coming out more and more.

"You don't squeeze ticks." Ronald says as he tries to adjust his body in his straps with only his left hand.

"I thought you put oil on ticks? Don't they breathe behind their heads?" Rod says.

"He wasn't being literal. He is just country!" Carla says with a laugh and looks over her shoulder at Shawn.

"Everyone we are five minutes from dropping out so be ready." Slill says and the tone of the engines starts to change.

Manual and Cash make their way down the hallway towards the room.

"Wow! That was a slap. That senorita has some fuego!" Manual says with a little more strut in his step.

"Manual, this is a possible business acquaintance. So I need you to remember that. You have that Shakespearean look in your eyes." Cash says with a smile looking down at the shorter man.

"Which play? Romeo and Juliet?" Manual says as they stand in front of the door.

"More like the three companions of Love's Labour's Lost." Cash says and knocks on the door. The play he mentioned leaves Manual perplexed, but before he can ask the door opens.

In front of him is the deliverer of the slap.

"Hello, Mr. Cashmere and Mr. Ramirez. I am Rosalie Hernandez and please come in." Rosalie says and has changed into jeans and a long sleeved t-shirt. She is wearing

Adidas sneakers and a hair is pulled into a loose bun. Cash hears Manual inhale next to him.

They enter the room and the other two ladies have changed into similar outfits. Both are on their feet with hands outstretched. Introductions are made and they are Lulu and Carolina Hernandez.

"So all of you are sisters?" Manual says as he takes them all in.

"Of course. Lulu is the oldest and Carolina is the baby. We were surprised to hear from Corey." Rosalie says.

"Wish I got the chance to slap him too." Lulu says with a giggle.

Chapter 40

Zinghavi

The last four jumps occurred with little to no incident. The weightlessness eliminated the pressures from wormhole transitions. Only one person activated the shot and that honor went to Shawn. Accidently discharging his syringe on the second to last jump by trying to shift positions in his seat right before the gravity was turned off. He is slowly coming back into consciousness.

"Shawn, can you hear me? You have been snoozing for a while, mate." Ronald asks as he stares down at Shawn as he stops and starts snoring. Rod and Carla left the bridge earlier to get ready for landing on Zinghavi in the next hour. Shawn suddenly snaps awake.

"What happened? How long have I been sleeping?" Shawn says and attempts to get up. Ronald presses his hands on Shawn's shoulders to keep him from doing so.

"You have been sleeping for the last two hours. Apparently sleeping is a task you try to avoid." Ronald says and watches Shawn reaction. There is fear in his eyes of not knowing what happened. Shawn unbuckles and stays in his seat. Ronald takes a seat in his chair and rotates it to face him. Taking his hands and scrubbing his face to continue waking up. The only other people or alien is Slill at the controls.

"I have memories, dreams or nightmares. Pretty much a whole mashup of all three. I sleep just not peacefully sometimes."

"Well, Sir. That is a burden we all have. I just wanted to make sure you were not waking up in a strange environment. There was no screaming or such. Physical manifestations such as the fists and a couple of swings."

"Thanks for waiting. You said we are an hour out?"

"That is correct. Go take a shower and change into your suit. We don't know what type of welcome Ool can expect."

"Well, you don't have to worry about that. We are not landing in the open or going anywhere to be seen today. In preparation for our arrival one of our contacts prepared a landing space outside of any major city. Also, we have been missing for months and have to reintroduce ourselves to our colleagues." Ool says as he nervously smooths his vest and stares out into his home world. There is an anticipation in his voice with an underlying tone of fear. The others radiate with a giddiness as they would jump out of the ship right now to dive into the cobalt water below. Shawn picks up on that fear and asks.

"Ool, you okay? You seem kinda of nervous." Shawn says as he grabs alcohol wipes and bandages to remove the IV ports. He starts with Rod and removes the port and cleans the area. He wraps it as well as Rod is transfixed looking at the city below sway and roll with ocean below it.

"The reason he is nervous is that the last time he was here, they attempted to kidnap him. After that probably would have killed him. He is a wanted man." Prill says as he continues to preen his top feathers with some sort of oil. All human faces focus on Ool as his feathers lose color and shivers at the memory. As they all absorb this information there is a feeling of being duped into working for the wrong side.

"Ool, now tell me the truth are you a criminal or not?" Ronald asks as he rubs his bandaged forearm.

"No. I am not a criminal, however I trusted a "friend" that is a criminal. I found out the truth when they ambushed me as I was retrieving the information to get in touch with you. They will definitely try to kill me once I am seen just to find out what I have done."

"So that means we will not be laying low after all. We get to play babysitter and possibly meet the enemy." Carla says as she pats Ool on his back just to reassure him.

"We will always have your back plus I need to stretch my legs anyways." Rod says as he heads back towards the quarters to get ready. He is soon followed by the rest of the crew to get ready as well.

Each person dons their neuro suit and armored suit sans the helmet. During the journey here the familiarity is innate and they are soon ready and head back to the bridge. The view of both the planets joined together by body of asteroids in the form of a tunnel is quite extraordinary. The planet Zinghavi is almost totally blue as oceans are infrequently broken up by land masses. Those masses are surrounded by light form the cities. Orenthia is a smaller planet that looks arid even from space and its water masses are concentrated at the pole areas of the planet. Once on the bridge the enormity of what they have stepped in is apparent as they see other ships passing by them. Slill guides the ship flawlessly outside of the city and heads out over the cobalt blue sea with ice dotting the waves.

"What's that creature off the port side?" Carmen asks as all heads swivel to see a cream colored row of dorsal fins knifing below them towards group of tear shaped specs in formation. The collision off both creature and formation is a sight to behold. The fins submerge and the creature attacks from beneath, however the tear shapes rocket skyward all except one. As the jaws of the creature close around it the "prey" elongates and wraps around the jaws trapping the maw in an open position in the jaw.

"The larger creature is an Artoo and the smaller is an Osk. The Artoo is very how can I say is "dumb". They always attack the Osk, but if they are not quick the Osk can trap them, look." Laz says and they all watch as the Artoo flounders and fights to close its jaws. The entire time water pours into its open mouth and the floundering slows then ceases. As the gigantic beast starts to roll and submerge the remaining Osk enter the mouth of the great beast. There is a collective gasp from the human cadre as the body of the Artoo ripples with activity.

"They are eating it. Wow! Talking about turning the tables." Rod says as the cobalt sea is tinged green from the blood leaving the Artoo in small geysers. Slill wings the ship over what seems an older part of the city. Buildings are quite a bit older and there is no activity in the air on the street. Taking the ship lower they enter a river that is running between the ocean and a smaller lake. He skillfully weaves through the moored anchors and raises the ship into an open pool. Once they surface they are bathed in lights.

"Welcome to your home." Ool says as he sees Lintoo standing alone with hope etched in his stance.

Chapter 41

Quite Pickled

"There is nothing quite like a perfectly tailored suit." Cash whispers to himself as he and Lulu ride the elevator up to their meeting. He admires the work of the Cuban tailor he frequented in Miami since arriving to America. The charcoal grey suit with light flecks of black heavier tones in the jacket and a shade lighter in the trousers. The vest and pocket square was opposite in black with charcoal grey flecks.

"You are quite dapper." A trio of female voices say in his ear. One in the elevator and two in his earpiece. He has to smile to himself as he forgot about the communication device in his ear. Lulu in her own right is also quite stunning. She is wearing a navy pants suit with light pin stripes with a pink blouse with a flourish at her neck line. Her hair is pulled into a tight twist with modest pearl studs.

"Any activity on the destination floor?" Lulu asks as the floors continue to pass by.

"No activity. Just a receptionist and staff moving around." Rosalie says in their earpiece perched across the street in a hotel penthouse. Corey was with her watching the street to verify exit routes are clear and no unexpected visitors. Manual and Carolina are one block to the south with Manual flying a low visibility drone as over watch.

"We are clear Mr. Cashmere." Manual says from the backseat of Ford Expedition with Carolina in the driver's seat. Both are dressed in casual gear, but armed to the teeth. Back up weapons in storage in the trunk for the others. The decision to take the meeting and be ready was made after surveillance. This was more than a mole hunt, it was a staged violent takeover. Taking place on US soil. The CEO has been on the winning end of two assassinations. The first was a car bomb and the second a cement truck. Both were amateur in nature and discreet as a baseball bat. The last thing Cash

wanted to be is caught unprepared on a third attempt.

"Arriving at the floor." Lulu says and then smiles as

the door opens onto a magnificent reception area. The office

was nothing but glass and chrome. There are hardwoods

running throughout and there is energy in the air. They

approach the receptionist who stands and comes around her

desk to shake hands.

"Welcome, Mr. Cashmere and Ms. Garcia (Lulu's

alias). Mr. Steinbeck is waiting for you in his office." The

receptionist says and promptly turns and guides them

through the offices. Past the door there is activity that all had

missed. There are ten gunman sitting in an office at the

ready.

"Seems there is a lot of security here, Ma'am. Are we

necessarily needed if he is this prepared?" Lulu asks

innocently and hears the click in her ear that acknowledges

the team got it. As they click across the floor towards the Mr.

Steinbeck the offices are empty along his corridor. The

receptionist is a Hispanic woman in at least her mid-forties

and in decent shape. She is wearing a pleated green skirt and

ivory blouse.

"Excuse me, Miss. You never shared your name with

my associate and I?" Cash says as he slows and waits for her

to turn around. Lulu passes Cash and places the briefcase she

is carrying on the ground. The receptionist stiffens as she

realizes her mistake. Then with alarming speed she fires a

rear side kick in the assumed direction of Cash. The counter

strike from Lulu is even faster and the assassin's plant leg

knee is shattered outward. Lulu dropped beneath the kick

and fired her own to the limb with surprising efficiency. As

the lady drops in agony, Cash clips her chin with his perfectly

polished dress shoe and she is unconscious. Lulu searches

her and removes three knives from various areas. They place her in an office and tie her up.

"I prefer not to hit a lady, but chivalry will not be the death of me. Third attempt is in play. Make sure we have a way out. Headed to Steinbeck's office." Cash says as Lulu pops the bottoms on the briefcases and assembles the sub-machine guns. She places a silencer on each and hands one to Cash. She then changes from the heels she has on to Adidas slip on running shoes.

"So I see you also brought a change of shoes for the occasion." Cash says with a smile and removes his jacket as well.

"Looks like the client in his fear has isolated himself and does not know that he is in danger. How are we looking outside?" Lulu says at the same time taking point down the hallway.

"Still quiet from up top. Do you need us to close in?" Carolina asks after Manual gave her the all clear sign as he maneuvered the drone in an expanding perimeter.

"Yes. Could you come to at least a street away on the building's North side?" Cash asks as they make their way to the only solid wall on the floor with Steinbeck's name on the door.

"I don't see you on the infrared. I lost you once you followed her in. So pretty much I am blind up here, so I am getting closer." Rosalie says. Then in turn starts to pack up her rifle.

"No. Hold your position. If the situation gets prickly, we will need support. Corey, you are in play. Head up and sit in the lobby. There are ten shooters past the inside door. Do not know if they are good or bad, so stay prepared either way." Cash says and tests the door knob. Once the door is cracked he hears someone on the phone. As they peek

347

through the door they see a man in a headset facing away

from them. He is looking out of the window deep in

conversation. They both enter and fan to the left and right.

Cash clears his throat and the man spins quickly.

Chapter 42

Warming Up

The unloading of the material was very uneventful. They were prudent in how the stores were dispersed. One third was left here in the new base, one third on the ship and the remaining would be left at a fall back stronghold. The equipment was also divided in the same manner. Shawn takes the atmospheric test and gets everyone together for the results while Ool and the new alien talk.

"Okay, the good news is the air is breathable for short durations. The Co2 is 400 million parts per million. An average on Earth is 350 parts per million. Meaning we can suffocate will prolonged exposure especially if we exert ourselves. This should be displaced by the higher oxygen content, but I would rather be safe than sorry." Shawn says as they stand on the dock beneath a huge building. Everything is modern according to their standards. Moving the equipment they noted that their quarters were shorter in height. Those adjustments were handled by Rod and a Zinghavi cutting torch.

"So we can breathe in an emergency?" Carla says as she readjusts her helmet. Prior to deploying they decided against compressed air tank and instead a scrubber air unit. The scrubber unit takes CO_2 and converts to oxygen. Placing it within the exterior suit thigh area to keep it out of harm's way.

"Hopefully, it will not come to that. Now we will have to seal our living quarters and set up the larger air unit so we can some comfort." Ronald says but stops as Ool and the others approach. The new one, Lintoo is similar in height to Ool, however his colors are brighter than Laz. He has an authority that has subdued the others. The stance they have is a sign that things are more complicated.

"Ronald, Carla, Rod and Shawn, thank you. This is such a great help to our people. The absence of these four was quite a stir a cycle back. However, now the more oppressive nature of the Orethians has become worse. There numbers have increased in occupancy on the planet. So my suggestion would be for these four should make a public reappearance first. Splitting them up would be more dangerous. What are your thoughts?" Lintoo finishes and takes a literal step back to allow them to speak. Ronald takes his time and has a thought that will change the future direction of Pearl Security.

"Carla, what are your thoughts?" Ronald asks and all heads turn from him to Carla.

"Why in the world are you asking me?"

"In reality you out rank all of us. I have no problem being number two. So what will it be Captain?" Ronald says and everyone could tell he is smiling under his helmet. After regaining her composure Carla slipped into the number one role seamlessly.

"Just the fact that he has a target on his back many would assume he would sneak into town. So they are watching his home and job, probably even Lintoo's home. Is anyone familiar with the relationship of Ool and Slill, Laz and Prill?" The four shake their heads simultaneously.

"So a definite know. Slill fly Laz and Prill to two different airports or whatever you call them and drop them off. Laz and Prill make your way home then to dinner with your usual friends. Give the story of being somewhere with a long work assignment. Slill fly back here from a different direction." Carla says and let the audience absorb this information.

"Understand, Carla. We will head out now." Slill waves for Laz and Prill to follow him. No handshakes or good-byes since this is just the beginning. Slill and crew load

up then submerge and disappear into the ocean.

"Now. What is the highest profile places that would

provide enough witnesses and enough cover to keep you two

safe?" Carla asks as the engine sounds fade into the water.

As they both ponder the question she takes a look at their

uniforms. They have a black matte finish with heavier plating

on the torso and flanks down to the hips. The leg plates are

less bulky as the arms are as well. Helmets with the fin on

the crown that holds cameras at different angles even in the

rear and fed to the display in the helmet.

"Well I feel the Saractac Towers casino would be the

ideal place. Several ways in and out. It has large crowds and

in the middle of the city." Lintoo says quite proud of himself

then a realization of what we means.

"I cannot go in there with you. I have to stay away

from this. If they know I have been with you or working with you I die! My entire family will die!" Lintoo screams as his

plumage feathers glow an intense red.

"Calm down, Lintoo. You will not be going in with Ool,

right?" Rod says and looks expectantly at Carla.

Without missing a beat.

"You will not be going in with Ool. You will be there,

but earlier than Ool. You will leave prior to him getting there

so you will be cleared when he makes his reappearance.

Now, could you go get the vehicle so we can survey the area

and have a rescue plan in order?" Carla says and walks away

with the others in tow.

"So Carla is the boss now?" Shawn asks quietly as they

head to the living quarters.

"We are soldiers and we know how leadership works.

Carla here outranks all of us. Just because the quid we will earn is quite a bit more, we will work like we are trained." Ronald says in his somber British lilt.

Mr. Steinbeck's eyes are wide as he looks down the barrels of both guns. His hands are flared out from his sides and headset still in place. Cash lowers his gun and Lulu turns to watch the door. Cash signals to mute the call.

Yes what is it? Who are you?" Steinbeck says with a shaky voice. He then ends the call with no explanation to whoever was on the only end. He is in his fifties and seems to be in good shape. Shorter than Cash with a sparse shock of gray hair on a tanned head.

"How long have you been back here? Did you notice anything on your way in here today?" Lulu asks with her back to him and knowing that time was not on their side.

"Got here? I have been here for days. Still who are you?"

"We are Pearl Security Consultants and I am Mr. Ronald Cashmere III. We had a meeting today." Steinbeck's face slackens into relief as reality sinks in. Then his face breaks into a grin.

"I am so glad you are here! They are trying to kill me. Where is my assistant Shamira?"

"Is she Hispanic?" Lulu asks.

"No. She is African-American. Why?"

"Hopefully, she got delayed at home. If not she may be deceased. The assassins have taken over your office and are waiting to set us up for your death. Do you have a security team here?" Cash asks as starts to examine the office windows for a vantage point. Looking out of the window he sees the truck a block over.

"My security team is five men at the patrolling the halls. Where are they?"

"Dead too. There are ten inside the front door waiting to kill all of us. This really sucks."

"Sorry to disappoint you Lulu. It has gotten quite a bit worse." Cash says as he sees three SUVs empty on the street below. Watching the crew disembark from the vehicles there is an additional count of twelve more potential assailants.

Chapter 43

A Sticky Wicket

"Mr. Cashmere, I think we need to get moving. It has been a few minutes and our crippled host has not checked in. So they are going to be coming here soon." Lulu says and checks the hallway once again.

"Give me a moment. Mr. Steinbeck this is not your typical "corporate" takeover. Why is everyone trying to kill you? Now let us know now and we will be on our way. If not you can handle this hornet's nest that is brewing." Cash says as he listens to Corey signal he has made it to the office. Manual checks in as well in at his position. Mr. Steinbeck face shifts color to a paler white than his office lifestyle has given him.

"It's not just about money. I married the right woman from the wrong family. They are from Venezuela and they want me out for them to takeover. I will not give up all my hard work! They want to use my business as a front and use my countermeasure defenses in their other businesses." Mr. Steinbeck's says and looks dejected.

"Cash, ask him why a thermal scope won't work on his building?" Cash acknowledges the question and repeats it to Mr. Steinbeck.

"That is one of the countermeasures I have developed. The building floor on this level has micro-jets installed underneath. There is a program linked to a server that pipes in hot and cool air in frequency to imitate a person walking, running or even sitting. It is a camouflage that keeps forces at bay. It is effective deterrent from raids."

"So can you shut the program down?" Lulu asks as she peers down the hallway and immediately tucks her head back.

"Do we have guests coming?" Cash asks. He looks and waits for the word from Mr. Steinbeck. Mr. Steinbeck nods and clicks a series of codes on his watch.

"I don't know what happened, but everything is clear. The staff has disappeared. I see you and a third person to the East. There is a large group heading from the West. I am counting ten." Rosalie says as she sights her rifle and loads a "heavy" to clear the path. A heavy is shell with an explosive ring behind the point of the bullet. The bullet will not penetrate fully, but will stick and the explosive will blow in the window to keep debris inside and also as projectiles.

"Heads up. Closing forces are headed up the South and the North. They are closing in on you. What's the play?" Manual asks as the drone sits over the top of the adjoining building.

"Corey, where are you?" Cash asks as he is calculating what needs to happen next.

"In the lobby. Ready." Corey calls back.

"We're going through to you." Cash says and points two fingers to the door.

After getting some sleep the four wake up for a meal of steak, instant potatoes and three cans of green beans. The common area was similar to any other forward camp with better bunks. Each person goes through their own calisthenics to get used to the gravity or the lack thereof. After a grueling hour long workout, they each take a shower and suit up. They make their way being led by Ool to the upper levels and wait under the cover of shadow. The street is deserted and Lintoo arrives in a van looking vehicle floating about two feet above the surface.

"Welcome again my friends. Let us be off." Lintoo says and pulls the vehicle off down the road. The vehicle seats are different than those of Earth. Instead of seating as a bench or captain chairs they are circular in nature and everyone is facing each other. Shawn takes the opportunity

to turn his away so he can see out of the window. What he

sees is more tangible than the first flyover just a day ago. The

activity is picking up around them and he sees other

Zinghavian. They as a race have so many colors and plumage

on their heads it reminds him of Carnival in Brazil. Also, he

sees his first kid Zinghavi. They do not have the colorful

plumage as their "parents" their feathers are all a soft blue

and seem to match the water that surrounds the city. Also,

there seems to be an amazement of their surroundings as the

"parents" have to keep them in tow constantly.

"Ool, can I ask you a question about your race?"

Shawn asks as he watches an adult lead the child along. The

child has color but not as bright. It is quite slimmer than the

adults.

"Of course, Shawn. What is it you may need to

know?"

"How is your race born? Your feathers and anatomy is similar to birds on Earth."

"Well, you take a female and a male with some Barry White." Rod says with a crescendo of laughs from his teammates.

"Who is this Barry White?" Lintoo asks as he maneuvers the vehicle over an expansive bridge on floating platforms. This question creates more laughter to extinguish the nerves on this insane expedition. The lights, the movement and all of the newness of their situation has everyone on edge.

"Now to answer your question. We are a bred species. There are similarities to your avian species called birds. We pro-create as other races, however when a potential hatchling is conceived they are delivered to a brood to be cared for. Once they are hatched the parents retrieve them to raise them." Ool says then points out of the side portal.

"That is a Zinghavi."

All eyes look at the group of them standing against a vehicle. They are more massive in person than on video. They top seven feet and are broad. Their skin is plated but not scaled as a lizard. The skin under their vest arm pits is not armored, but seems pliable for movement.

"Only thing is missing is a tail. They definitely look like lizards." Carla says and starts typing on the arm mounted PDA. Each person has one mounted and it tracks all data with entries. Ronald who has made the effort not to force leadership his way and slowly back away to let Carla run the team.

"The joints are the key to this wicket. Now if they look pliable, what is the possibility of penetration to the softer parts?" Ronald says as a possible plan evolves in his head.

Carla simply nods in his direction and they both are on the

same page.

Lintoo stops the vehicle in front of a massive building

with lines of people on the street.

"Welcome to Saractac Towers. The casino is five

levels and there is a private room in the back that we access

to have privacy." Lintoo says.

"Keep driving so I can launch our drone to get details."

Carla says as she opens the drone case to prep for flight. As

they are moving the roof slides back and the drone is

powered up. With a silent hum the drone rockets away into

the night. The scanning camera begins shooting images to all

PDAs and main computers.

Chapter 44

Cordite and Earaches

Hearing the message from Cash, Corey sets up to give his Uncle, Lulu and the client a clear exit. Making his way into the lobby with no resistance, Corey sets up to lay out a red carpet.

"Hey, who are you?" An armed man with a partner on the other side of the lobby glass. They both are a full head smaller than he is, but both have M-16 rifles and Kevlar. Both seem calm so he will play calm.

"Easy. Easy brother. I am just a driver. My passengers were supposed to be at the curb over thirty minutes ago, so I came up." Corey says with his hands out from his side. His heavy gun is at the bag at his feet, but he has two 40 caliber pistols under his jacket. As they consider what they should do the window behind them explodes and sends them flying towards him. Corey shoots the two knives under each sleeve out and plunges them deep into the throats of the airborne assailants.

"Thanks for the assist. It's time to get grimy!" Corey yells and grabs the heavy gun and a couple of surprises. He makes his way through the smoke and listens to his earpiece.

"No problem Corey. You have eight in the hallway straight ahead of you. Four are splitting off and headed back towards you and the other four are pushing to you Sir." Rosalie says and she loads another heavy in the chamber.

As Corey rounds the corner he sees the forms of soldiers headed his way. Equipped with a silencer his FN P90 with expanded clip loaded with hollow points. He pumps rounds into the lead man with barely audible pops that are hidden by the fire alarms. As he drops he is on to the next before return fire comes from his compatriots. Shots pepper the wall where Corey was standing, however laying on the ground he unleashes another volley into their abdomens and legs. The screams and shouts from the tearing of bullets and slow death soon clears the way.

"Four down. Your turn Lulu." Corey says as he cleans up the mess and clears the path.

Carmen flies the drone with ease. Several bird like creatures fly around observing this strange new beast. The scans show that the tower is built with the phez beams. However the difference is the windows or the lack thereof. The openings do not have windows, but are open air. They have an entrance, but now the question that is in the back of her mind.

"Carla. We will have to make some test firing before we attempt anything." Ronald says while looking at her.

"That is exactly what I was thinking. Let us get some more data, shall we." Carla says and loop to the rear of the building.

"Stop there! Look at the doors in the rear. The alley is pretty narrow, but there is catwalk across to the eighth floor. We can stage in that building then work over that way. Over watch can hold cover on our exit." Shawn says as the glowing catwalk continue to fill in with more scan data downloaded. It was good that each person had input.

"What we need to do is engage one. I rather do it in the open than enclosed with a crowd. Nothing like getting your teeth possibly getting kicked in with a crowd. So let's combine two activities, test fire and scout?" Rod says with a yawn.

"Sounds fun. Bringing the bird back and we will go stir up some trouble." Carla says with a knowing shake of her head. This is what she will have to deal with testosterone and a sense to prove who is the toughest. She would certainly oblige any man that had to prove it. Reality is a necessary evil.

After packing the drone up in its case. Lintoo heads towards another section of town nearer the water and looks like a warehouse area. There are Orethians working the pier are pushing floating carts of materials. Loading the pallets to a larger crane loading area to be loaded onto a vessel. Sitting there in the vehicle they just wait.

"What are we waiting for?" Shawn says with a yawn and leans back into his seat. The sound of the ocean and movement is a soothing sound and they are tired from space travel and a new planet. As if on cue four Zinghavi come onto the pier riding on a similar floating vehicle with no top. They are massive and all carry some sort of sword and a rifle. They disembark and one heads in the direction of a building. The remaining three pass around a block of something and begin to chew.

"Rod, are you sure you want to do this? We could watch them for a little while to check them out. This could be a short deployment for you if you guess wrong." Shawn says as Rod and Carla prepare to leave. Rod's face is hidden, but his body language becomes more defiant as if he is weak.

"You are not being called out. This is an unknown right now and we should take it slow." Ronald says and gets no response as Rod grabs the door handle. Without a word being said, Rod and Carla slip out of the van and scoot through the shadows. Rod was going to show them how good he is. Ronald, Shawn, Ool and Lintoo remain in the van to watch the other three.

"What are the chewing?" Ronald asks as the three remain motionless as they chew. Ool's feathers lose color and he answers.

"It is an opioid from our salt from the sea. This has been mixed with various chemicals and flesh."

"Whose flesh?" Ronald asks and knowing the answer already has his solidify his anger.

"They get from our breeder house from failed hatchlings." Ool says with a groan.

Lulu pushes through the door and checks the hallway left and right then signals to follow her. They head back down the hallway with Cash in the rear. Surprisingly, there are no smoke alarms or sprinklers with the smoke in the hallway ahead. This far down the hallway the smoke is ankle level. Sweeping eyes left and right Lulu gets them close to where there first assailant is restrained, hopefully.

"Cash, watch that door." Lulu whispers with her head nodding to the left while she sidles closer to her right. As if she could see through walls, the door flies open and the killer lunges out with another blade, but hits nothing but air. The strike more of a desperate lunge leaves her exposed to a double tap to the back of her head to the horror of Mr. Steinbeck.

"Who was that?!" Mr. Steinbeck yells as he jumps back into Cash. Cash in turn shoves him into the open door. Shots start to pepper the drywall as the four assailants round the corner at the end of the hallway. Lulu and Cash return fire as they take shelter in offices across from each other. The body in the hall bucks with movement as bullets hit it in the throes of involuntary muscle movement. Cash and Lulu continue to shoot and are rewarded by a shout signaling they were successful in hitting one. Then they get one in return as Lulu falls back with bullet to her upper chest near her shoulder. She falls with a grunt, but holds a hand up to keep Cash in his place.

"I'm okay. The bullet hit the vest, but it still hurts. I won't be able to wear a bikini for a while." Lulu says with a weak smile.

"That would be a shame." Mr. Steinbeck says unconsciously while in shock. That comment earns him another weak smile and Lulu reaches her hand out. Steinbeck pulls her to her feet as the gunfire continues. A heavy chatter of a larger gun can be heard as another one falls.

"Lulu, you had one job and you get shot! Now I have to bail you out again!" Corey hisses in concert with the thudding of the rifle. One more body drops from Corey and Cash clips the last one as he finally understands the end. The hallway falls silent with the exception of remaining gasps of the nearly dead and the ringing of their ears.

"You couldn't put a silencer on that cannon." Cash says as he takes a look at Lulu and ensures Mr. Steinbeck is in one piece.

"I had one, but I removed it for the dramatic affect. The awe and shock bought you the gate way to freedom, right. Now we still have to get downstairs and out." Corey says as their radios once again relay news.

Chapter 45

Keep Your Hands Up

"Rod, do you really want to do this?" Carla asks as they sit in the shadows watching their quarry lock up the building he was in for about thirty minutes. The Orethian was at least a foot and half taller than Rod. Also, twice as large. This could be a very huge problem literally. Rod standing in his suit seems pretty intimidating. Over the months he had put on at twenty-five pounds of muscle and seemed ready. Ready is a relative term.

"We can back out and handle this a better way? Let's go back. I was curious if they are as large as they seemed. They are huge and dropping them from distance is smarter." Carla implores Rod, but knows if she orders him back that this will cause an issue later.

"You worry too much. I got this. You just back me up from over here." Rod says then heads in the direction of his opponent. Each of them had the modified side arm that has not been test fired, however each had the compact razor bow with the phez tipped arrows and a combat knife tipped with it as well. Rod stays in the shadows and walks directly on the side of the passageway where the Orethian has to pass to leave. As the Orethian gets closer, Rod steps into his path. Fortunately, he is aware enough to have his camera live streaming this encounter where everyone can see.

"What is this? What are you?" The Zinghavi stutters and looks at Rod in surprise. Apparently, a human popping out from nowhere has him truly unbalanced. As Rod looks up at him the entire team takes a collective gasp. Rod says nothing, but goes on the offensive with a kick to the groin of the beast who falls back in amazement then pain.

"Rod, this is Ool. The genitalia of Orethian is retractable such as an amphibian like a turtle." There is a subtle tremor in all male occupants and a laugh from Carla.

While everyone is relaxed there is shout as the Zinghavi takes

the offensive and lunges at Rod with an overhead strike that

Rod blocks. The power of this beast causes Rod to rumble a

low curse. As the beast winds up for another blow, Rod

shoots a kick to the soft flesh where a knee is supposed to be.

The joint bends backwards and the blow the beast throws still

comes with no loss of power, which is blocked as well.

"Rod, its Ool again. They are also double jointed since

they have to climb rocky surfaces on their world."

"Ool! You need to give us all the information at once!

Not when I am trying to keep my head attached!" Rod yells

on internal microphone. So that means the water is getting

deeper and Rod goes on the offensive. Getting to his feet

Rod goes to the body with successive hooks which causes the

Orethian to rock back. Once he goes back, Rod presses

forward with another combination to the head to the body

and back to the head. The loaded gloves making solid contact that drops the Orethian down to one double jointed knee. The gloves are loaded with lead to give each punch a more solid concussive power. Not accepting this Rod takes a step back before the next wave from him. Calculating right the Orethian rushes him and is met with Muay Thai knee to its exposed face. This final blow elicits a laugh as the Zinghavi spits blue blood from his mouth. Rod is airborne in an instant and there is no pain just weightlessness.

"Rod, is in trouble! These things pack a punch!" Carla says in astonishment as she watches Rod float for a full two seconds before heading back to the ground.

"There are three groups heading your way. I count six in the elevator and six on each stairway." Rosalie calls out from her perch.

"We need to get some help to get out of this one. Any ideas?" Cash asks as they make their way to the lobby.

"Don't worry I got it. Be ready to move. There is a lot of activity on the street from spectators from the first heavy. I am bringing the drone over the alley right now, where they have their vehicles parked. It's away." Manual says as the drone shoots a flare in each of the open dumpsters on either side of the alley. They instantly burst into flames and black smoke floods the street. Cellphones are calling 911 and taking pictures. Fire engines can be heard from the station a mile away.

"They are pulling back." Rosalie says. All of the opposing teams leave the building and load up in their vehicles. Police contact is not what any hit squad does not want. Sirens are blaring and people are pouring out of buildings on either side of Mr. Steinbeck's. Four people ease into the chaos. Their weapons all in Corey's bag and Lulu wearing Cash's jacket to cover her bloody shirt. They get into the vehicle with Manual and Carolina to merge into traffic as the fire trucks arrived.

"Rosalie, we have them. Meet us back at the airstrip." Lulu says with a grunt as she tries to get comfortable. They were packed in pretty tight with the four of them not including the massive form of Corey. Mr. Steinbeck was introduced to all in the vehicle as they made their way back to the airport. There was a roar of a motorcycle and determined Rosalie passed them with her hair flowing in the wind in the modified helmet.

"So what is the plan Mr. Cashmere?" Manual asks from the passenger seat.

"First there will be a discussion and finalization of our contractual obligations and emergency intervention." Cash says as he straightens out his cuff links without making eye contact with Mr. Steinbeck.

"I feel the initial fee of two hundred and fifty thousand plus expenses with a thirty percent emergency intervention fee." Corey says from the passenger seat without turning around. They pass over the causeway without any interference.

"I agree to pay the fee. What about my family?" Mr. Steinbeck says with fear in his voice. The fatigue tinges his voice as the adrenaline wanes on the drive.

"Took the liberty to tuck them away when I realized you were compromised. They are tucked away in Cuba with our family. Our family will watch them and they will be a lot happier after this vacation. You will be too." Carolina says from behind the wheel. As they reach the airport there are two planes waiting. Cash and Manual get on their plane while Corey, the three sisters and Mr. Steinbeck board the second plane with Mr. Currie. Mr. Currie will make the drop and return commercially. Cash and Manual head back to

Texas with a ping to the offshore bank account with the first

installment from Mr. Steinbeck.

Chapter 46

Boogered Up

Rod tries to shake off the disorientation. There is not any pain, which is weird since he was hit by a Mack truck. There is no glitching in the head display, but he feels the ground beneath him.

"Must be that crazy sky with the two moons and the other planet hanging on with a glowing string." Rod mumbles and the image of an Orethian blocks out the view. The beast stares down at him with a blade and what he thinks is a smile. Then his head disappears with a blue mist. As he wipes the blood off of his visor he sees Carla standing there with her hand outstretched. He grabs it and gets him to his feet.

"What happened?" Rod says groggily as his legs get their strength back.

"You didn't keep your hands up and got too cocky! This thing knocked you in the air and you landed on your head. The suit protects from high impact projectiles and explosions, but does not have the integrity to protect against falls or crashes. We have to get out of here!" Carla says as she puts his arm over her shoulder to help him back to the shadows.

"We are almost there!" Ronald says as they skirt around the group and head to help.

"No, I have him. Stay with Ool." Carla says as Rod's legs get stronger. She knows he has a concussion and this is on her.

"Too late." Shawn says as they see them coming up. Both he and Ronald grab Rod from Carla.

"Ool, bring the vehicle around." Carla orders.

"Sorry, I cannot. Where are you taking us? Ool asks

and there is a scream of pain from Lintoo.

"We take you to Hurg and get our reward. He been

looking for you." The Orethian says in a drunken voice.

"So we will take you to the Saractac Towers so he can

deal with you and the other one." Another Orethian says as

the communications starts to breakdown due to interference

from the buildings. There are no words spoken and they all

know they have to get to the towers.

"Hopefully, I can get Slill to come get us?" Carla says

as she knows that the mission can end in a short time if Ool

dies. There is a garble on the line and Slill is informed of what

is going on. He assures them he will be there and they four

set off to get picked up at a better vantage point. They all

slowly make their way to the rally point to meet Slill. Rod

soon has his wits back and they make quick time through

alleys and shadows to the rally point. There are several

beasts similar to rats and scurry to find cover from the new comers. The size is similar to rats, but have scaled skins similar to lizards with glowing green eyes.

"Sorry about this." Rod says as they sprint through town.

"It is not all on you, but me. I should have not let you take that thing on alone." Carla says as she jumps the fence bringing up the rear.

"Okay, that is enough of us feeling sad about Ool. We will get him back. There needs to be a plan since we are going in cold. Slill how close are you?" Ronald says. Upon getting that answer Ronald pulls his sidearm and sights on the rat like creature and pulls the trigger. The gun recoils and there explosion of scales and skeleton.

"Guns work." Shawn says and grins.

"I have you on my scanner. Be there in one of your Earth minutes." Slill says in their ear pieces. They clear the last of the buildings and meet Slill in an opening in a park. They all board and start gathering gear for the rescue. A plan is soon formulated and they start for the Towers to grab Ool.

"Now I am to believe you have been here the entire time?" Hurg says as he drinks his purple drink in their private suite in the casino. Ool and Lintoo are unwilling guests as their feathers are mottled and sprinkled with their own blood. They are delivered more blows to punctuate the question.

"It is true and Lintoo has nothing to do with this. Let him go!" Ool says with his strongest voice. He knows he has to hang in just for the others to save him.

"We are here Ool. Keep it up. We will get to you." Ronald says as he sees the tower below. The plan according to the prints from the drone their access will be through the kitchen. Per the plan Rod will have over watch and back

them up since he is already banged up. Carla, Ronald and

Shawn will blitz through the kitchen using the element of

surprise. They drop a line from the rear of the ship and repel

to the access bridge they spotted earlier. Dropping onto the

landing they find the door motion activated. They move as a

group into the kitchen area.

"The scanner shows fifteen. Two in the kitchen and

ten in the main casino. Lastly, three in the rear room with

Ool and Lintoo I think. I have moved back and am hovering

on the far side near the holding lot. Get them back." Slill says

with the first concern they have ever heard.

They enter the kitchen and try to stay inconspicuous,

but the staff takes one look and run in fear. Thankfully the

Orethians are not looking at them, but are confused by all of

the confusion. The "chew" they use dulls their senses, but

not their reflexes. Carla and Shawn flank the two prep tables following behind the escaping Zinghavi while Ronald hangs back waiting for their next move. They spot Ronald and are confused by what they see. Before they can register each one fall in shock as both their armpits mist from synchronized shots from Carla and Rod. The shots are muffled since they are propellant discharged. This may not be too bad. They move to the door and look out of the windows in the door. On the other side the commotion in the kitchen has not reached the floor yet.

"We have no choice, but to hit hard and fast." Carla says. She surveys the potential issues of the Orethians in the way. As if reading her thoughts.

"Hopefully, if they see all the chaos they will get out of the way. Wish we had a fire alarm." Shawn says with hope in his voice.

Chapter 47

Wow

"No fire alarm, but we have this!" Carla says as she

hefts one of the sonic grenades. In one fluid motion she sets

the charge button cracks the door and tosses it in. The sonic

grenade emits a modulating tone that hurts and disorients.

Once the charge goes off there are screams and money hits

the floor as everyone grabs their ears and vomit

simultaneously. The Zinghavi scramble for the door as the

Orethians still try to get their feet under them. Carla, Ronald

and Shawn make their way through the chaos to get their

firing lanes.

"Rod, make your way in and set up in the upper

balcony. It's about to get crazy!" Carla says as she flips over a

gaming table and shoves a female Zinghavi towards the door.

The only reason she can tell she is a female is difference of

her clothing and slender build. There is a thud in the table next to her head and a concussive sound right behind it. This is the first shot from the enemy and it is serious.

"Taking fire and it bloody hurts!" Ronald says as he takes three concussive shots through his table. After the shot he tosses a magnetic field grenade to the center of the chaos. Orethians shake off their dismay and fire with no concern of lives around them. When the grenade levitates off the ground and hovers it starts to draw in all metal to the circumference of the field. Chips, knives and bullets are pulled in that direction. The field provides cover and disarms those in the vicinity. Needless to say as the surprise of Orethian gang there is an utter confusion among them. This creates a lull in the action where Ronald decides to press the offense.

The smell of Orethians in the air even through the filtered masks, leaves the team gasping. Orethians bodies produce an overwhelming putrid smell when they sweat. It is a combination of sulphur, vomit and rot.

A look at the surroundings the team is pinned down and he signals for them to press in the confusion. The ceramic bullets insulate the phez where the magnetic field is not effective against them. Shawn and he get into position to unleash a deadly crossfire that drops three more with explosions of blue. This firefight and its ongoing barrages has at least 20 Zinghavi dead intermingled with the roasted carcasses of 15 Orethian hit squad members.

Pinned down and still heavy on ammo the team waits on the signal from Flips, who is tracking the attackers on her wrist cam feed from the over watch balloon hidden in the chandelier. Ronald's combat suit is covered in remnants of two hit squad members who he is using as cover behind the Zinghavi version of a blackjack table. On his signal she hand gestures the return assault to cease they turn to rescuing their two comrades. All communications are jammed due to the floating masses of metal chips suspended in magnetic halo grenade fields.

Flanking right and left respectively, Ronald and Shawn scuttle around bodies and overturned tables to provide the pincers in the trident formation. Backing them from a higher vantage point behind them, Rod is setting up grenade launcher with phosphorous loads to melt and blind to push the remaining Orethians into the vice. Flip's hand counts down to one...

"Here it comes!" Rod says and fires. The round hits and the foreign concept of it presses them to get cut down. The phosphorous grenade also melts the halo grenade, which allows better visibility of the room. There is a shout and Ool with Lintoo make a run to where Shawn is laying down cover fire.

"Get behind me and make your way to the kitchen! I have Ool and Lintoo! Fall back!" Shawn says. As he begins to fall back three massive Orethians burst through the opening behind Ool and Lintoo. They begin to fire at three of the four. Carla, Shawn and Ronald do the same back at them, which cuts down one as a round hits home in exposed section of its neck. He falls and it causes some hesitation.

"I know not what these beings are. We must warn Ash." Hurg says and heads for a door. His last remaining ally follows right behind him. The shooting stops, although there are moans and groans from the wounded. Finally when the shooting stops, they here the bleating of something in the distance.

"Everyone! Let's bail before reinforcements get here!" Ronald roars as he clears himself out of the debris that was a pillar.

"Get to the roof. I am hovering two floors below the roof. Hurry!" Slill says and that spurs movement. Lintoo guides them to the tubes to get them to the roof. There are still Zinghavi hiding in shops and the menagerie of color is still overwhelming even in the pressure of what has happened. They reach the roof and make off with Slill with no resistance. The first impromptu mission was a success. Only injuries sustained are nothing more than bumps and bruises from

being shot. The armor holds exceptionally well, but the

soreness from successive blows leaves all wincing when

jostled.

"Good work, gents. Let's get back to base." Carla

says. As they wing away Ronald sends a message to his father

through the special encrypted device that beams to a

receiving device back on Earth.

Chapter 48

Sunshine

Cash slept for the entire flight back. He ached in all types of places, but he felt so alive after being in that booth for so many years. As they touch down he feels so good to be back in familiar surroundings, but he missed his son. The plane taxis to its hangar and they both disembark.

"Mr. Manual, thank you. Please let's take a couple of days off to get our wits back." Cash says as he gets his bags from the storage hold.

"No problem Sir. Would you mind helping me do the final checks before I park her?" Manual asks as he was exhausted as well.

"Sure."

This is quite a lovely home as she walks through the kitchen. Touching its immaculate granite countertops and bamboo floors as they click under her heals. There is a masculine aroma in the air. She walks in the office in the back of the house. The desk is immaculate and she admires

the view of the ocean. As she walks the hallway to towards

the other wing of the house she hums a song. Passing by the

first bedroom she finds the room she has been looking for.

"Well. Is this not just a Spartan space for a man?"

Dolores coos as she looks around Ronald's room. She runs

her fingers along his bed and avoids moving anything to keep

her visit discreet. Walking back to leave and not overstay,

she sees a flashing light coming from a night table in Mr.

Cashmere's room.

"Dolores. We need to be leaving, Ma'am. Have you

seen what is necessary?" Randall says as he stays stock still

and watching the door. They have two men outside plus one

in the truck. This place was beautiful compared to London,

but the blasted humidity leaves it quite miserable. She takes

a look and cannot stop smiling when she decides to come

back. As she leaves, Randall wipes down the knob and

relocks the door using a scrambler. The heat is like a wall and

they climb into the cool confines of the Escalade.

They pull out onto Ocean Drive and head towards the

airport to head back. Finding the Cashmeres was not easy,

but the picture of a motorcycle riding the barrier over the

Harbor Bridge. An onlooker snapped a picture and the side

view of Ronald Cashmere IV. So many ways to find him and a

teenager catches him. They pull out to see the ocean view

and wait for better timing.

Cash arrives back home and can't understand why he

smells lilacs. Nothing seems amiss and he heads to his room

to shower. His suit or what remains of it could be salvaged.

The smoke smell permeates the hallway and his bedroom

that masks the lilac smell in the house. Cash smiles as the

change of his life since nine months ago has allowed him to

feel more alive than he has in years. Entering his room he sits

back on his antique wood chair to slip off his shoes. His eyes

catches the blinking light in the bedside table. He opens the drawer and it's the communication device designed by Laz. It is similar to a satellite phone, but the difference is its holographic projector. He punches in his designated code and he sees Ronald's face.

"Hey, Pop. We got here safe. This place is so far beyond our imagination. Words cannot explain the majesty and there is no comparing it to anything on Earth. Carla has been instated as leader and I am the number two as we discussed. The enemy is quite formidable. Rod was the first to make contact and now he dealing with a concussion. That reality has sobered him up and I feel we had a better footing going on our first impromptu mission. Ool and Lintoo were taken hostage and we were successful in rescuing them. The suits worked superb, however their weapons pack more of a punch than what we anticipated. No one has been hurt critically, but we are bruised and battered. Pop, we will be successful. Don't forget to take your medications and do not get shot! I love you, Pop" Ronald says all of this from inside the helmet. Seeing his son decked out and communicated so calmly that his heart rate starts to slow.

Cash showers and shaves his head then trims his beard. Jazz is playing on the bedside radio as he just enjoys the quiet, which is soon interrupted. The doorbell rings and Cash ignores it initially as he has his straight razor underneath his jawline. As he wraps up and cleans his face the doorbell rings again. Exasperated he heads to the door, he grabs his Glock 17 and slips it beneath his robe in the waistband of his lounge pants. He also slips his straight razor in his robe pocket and heads for the door. He looks at the monitor and he sees Harold and Cassius standing there. He immediately opens the door.

"Harold and Cassius, me boy." Cash says and scratches Cassius under his chin. He also grabs Harold's two bags and they head into the house.

"Hello, Mr. Cashmere. We just got back from some banking tasks in the Caymans. I tried calling before I got on my flight." Harold says as they enter the living room and he stops suddenly as he bumps into the entry chair.

"Well, I missed the call while we were flying back in from Florida. What's wrong?" Cash asks as he sits the bags down and heads to put the kettle on. Cassius also is standing in the same place with a low growl as his head scans the area.

"Do you have company Mr. Cashmere?" Harold asks as he starts to move around now with Cassius leading the way.

"No, Sir. You would have known that once you entered the door. What is wrong, Harold?" Cash says alarmed and leaves the kettle in the sink.

"Well, someone has been here. There is a heavy aroma of lilac and an unfamiliar cologne as well. Also, someone moved the chair in the sitting area and that is why I ran into it." Harold says and Cash excuses himself to get dressed. He also makes an immediate text to Manual for his address. It was closer to get to Manual then the next move.

His home already being compromised left goosebumps along

his arms as he got dressed.

Chapter 49

Regroup

"Ool, you have to sit still." Shawn says as he is stitching the gash on Ool's cheek. All of the crew is banged up with the exception of Slill. Shawn for his work the last two hours consisted of assessing bone bruises, four broken fingers and numerous stiches on his human counterparts. Now he was attempting to patch up an alien and that in itself was exhilarating and terrifying. Their skin was thicker than human skin so the needle he used was designed for veterinarians. The clotting capacity was quite fascinating due to the fact it was instantaneous with each puncture.

"I used a regular filament stitch. Did not want to take a chance and the dissolvable stiches won't do that with your physiology? Now let me take care of the cut on your neck now." Shawn says and begins the next injury.

While Shawn is in his element patching up Ool and Lintoo, the others sit in the common area icing their injuries.

Rod is laying back on one of the couches with an ice bag on the top of his head for the concussion. He has two broken fingers on his left hand from the initial fight. Ronald is laying on the couch parallel to Rod with ice packs wrapped across his chest where the Orethian shells bruised him down to the rib cage. They are both listening to the determined, frustrated and elated tones of Carla during their mini-debrief. Shawn can hear since there are no doors installed at the base.

"Now we survived this, but we can be so much better. No look at them, they do not hide for cover when we fire. They are convinced they are impervious and that is where we can gain more ground. We have to tighten up our entries and formations." Carla says as she points out the running vid screen shots from each of their helmets. There are disorientating and loud with all the shouting and explosions. Carla stops on Ronald's camera before they retreated. The Orethian standing on the screen was taller than any of the ones they had seen so far. He has deep scarring and paint on his torso with Zinghavi feathers on his shoulder.

"That is Hurg "The Merciless", he is an underboss for Ash the Orethian leader. They have been looking for me and were going to kill me. If you did not come I would be dead. Thank you." Ool says with a bow. His clothing is spattered with his blood and probably Lintoo's as well. He is limping as well and his feathers are missing in random places. The look in his eyes and the hardness in the cones display a feral tenacity.

"Well before we can get to Ash, Hurg will have to die first. Ash has no reason to show himself if the underbosses are handling everything. Is Ash even real?" Rod says groggily still laying on his back. There is a somber tone in his voice that reality has set in. On paper this should have been straight forward, but the enemy is much harder than a 3D briefing.

"So the first order of business is to learn how to fight them the right way. We will not survive here long if we have missions like this. Can't be the bug on the windshield all the time?" Shawn says as he walks in with weariness in his stance, but a glimmer in his eye. On the outside Shawn may seem pedestrian in his manners, belies the warrior and the doctor within. There is an underlying fierceness and a viciousness that he struggles to contain.

"What does that mean, Shawn? A bug and a windshield?" Lintoo asks with an incredulous look with his bruised face and missing teeth. The look on his face was the literal meaning of the saying. There is no laughter as it sinks in.

"We have to be surgeons to cut this out. So there must be precision in our strikes and methods. No more solo initiatives to prove ourselves! We have to behave as a team and we follow Carla and he instructions with no wavering!"

Ronald says as he rises to his feet and each person comes out

of their own melancholy to understand.

"Precision means patience and planning. Now that we

see what we are dealing with this is will be eliminate with no

chance of return." Carla says as she closes screens and

uploads the drone data.

Upon arrival at Manual's house they were met by

Manual and all of his family members when the front door

was opened. This caught Cash and Harold unprepared and

before they know it they are sitting at the kitchen table

drinking coffee and eating Pan de Dulce. Manual's mother in

the kitchen cooking frijoles and chorizo. Cassius is laying on

his back getting his belly rubbed by Manual's niece and

nephew. Cash implored Mrs. Ramirez that would not be

necessary and she just smiled and headed to the kitchen.

Manual parked the Range Rover in his garage and swept it for

a tracker as well.

"So you smelled something different in the house? Can you tell how long a smell can be in the air? Manual asks as he pours cream in his coffee. He is dressed in a t-shirt and jeans with his hair slicked back. The scars along his face and neck are red swollen due to the excessive heat. The scars are his and to say what happened is also on him.

"Mr. Manual, I know I smelled something. Cassius smelled it as well and it had him worked up. Now the time they were there was recent. Smells dissipate over time especially with air flow from the central unit. It was a lady and a two men definitely. This is some good coffee, Mrs. Ramirez." Harold says as he sips his coffee then tips it in salute to the sounds in the kitchen. She just smiles and waves her hand not understanding that he is blind.

Cash sips his coffee and grimaces. Tea was more his forte and coffee was just too strong in America.

"Well, it seems that a quite prickly discretion that happened upon Ronald and I." Cash said as the food was served. The tortillas, beans and chorizo are absolutely divine.

While they eat Cash retells the story of the parking garage

and all things related. The only omission was of their

benefactors. After the retelling they sit there and just finish

eating in silence as they all speculate.

"Well, we are going back to your house and I will set it

up. My cuñado is an electrician and we will use his truck as

cover. We will secure it and then we will deal with everything

else. When will Corey be heading back?" Manual asks as he

finishes sending a text message.

"So you and your brother-in-law will do this for us? I

appreciate that. Corey is coming in tomorrow and Steinbeck

is secure with the ladies. I appreciate the hospitality and is

there something Mrs. Ramirez or your family needs let me

know." Cash says as he wipes his mouth and stands to

embrace her hand at the last of his statement. After

pleasantries Harold and Cash are headed to the door after

Cassius. As they are saying their final good-byes, Cassius

unleashes a low growl. They all turn their attention to him

then the street. On the street there are four men waiting

next to a black SUV. The back door opens and a well-dressed

gentlemen gets out with his a prosthetic on his left hand. He

makes his way up the sidewalk towards them in the muggy

night air.

"Evening, Mr. Cashmere and your associates as well. I

have one question for you. Where is the money?" Gus asks

and raises what is left of his left hand. Four assault rifles rack

at that precise moment and the night grows even more still.